# The Secret of Sigma Seven

"Eat photons, alien dog!" a voice suddenly shouted.

Simon Devoreaux, the movie director, froze in his tracks and stared toward the door in disbelief. Frank turned to see a person dressed like the hero of *The Secret of Sigma Seven* standing by the door. He wore black armor and a helmet that formed a mask over his face. His long black cape almost touched the floor.

Smiling maliciously, the armor-clad man pulled a zap gun out of his holster and pointed it directly at Devoreaux, who was stunned.

The man in black pulled the trigger on the gun. There was an exploding sound, and a bullet sped out of the muzzle directly at the startled director!

# The Hardy Boys Mystery Stories

#59  Night of the Werewolf
#60  Mystery of the Samurai Sword
#61  The Pentagon Spy
#62  The Apeman's Secret
#63  The Mummy Case
#64  Mystery of Smugglers Cove
#65  The Stone Idol
#66  The Vanishing Thieves
#67  The Outlaw's Silver
#68  Deadly Chase
#69  The Four-headed Dragon
#70  The Infinity Clue
#71  Track of the Zombie
#72  The Voodoo Plot
#73  The Billion Dollar Ransom
#74  Tic-Tac-Terror
#75  Trapped at Sea
#76  Game Plan for Disaster
#77  The Crimson Flame
#78  Cave-in!
#79  Sky Sabotage
#80  The Roaring River Mystery
#81  The Demon's Den
#82  The Blackwing Puzzle
#83  The Swamp Monster
#84  Revenge of the Desert Phantom
#85  The Skyfire Puzzle
#86  The Mystery of the Silver Star
#87  Program for Destruction
#88  Tricky Business
#89  The Sky Blue Frame
#90  Danger on the Diamond
#91  Shield of Fear
#92  The Shadow Killers
#93  The Serpent's Tooth Mystery
#94  Breakdown in Axeblade
#95  Danger on the Air

#96   Wipeout
#97   Cast of Criminals
#98   Spark of Suspicion
#99   Dungeon of Doom
#100  The Secret of the Island Treasure
#101  The Money Hunt
#102  Terminal Shock
#103  The Million-Dollar Nightmare
#104  Tricks of the Trade
#105  The Smoke Screen Mystery
#106  Attack of the Video Villains
#107  Panic on Gull Island
#108  Fear on Wheels
#109  The Prime-Time Crime
#110  The Secret of Sigma Seven
#111  Three-Ring Terror
#112  The Demolition Mission
#113  Radical Moves
#114  The Case of the Counterfeit Criminals
#115  Sabotage at Sports City
#116  Rock 'n' Roll Renegades
#117  The Baseball Card Conspiracy
#118  Danger in the Fourth Dimension
#119  Trouble at Coyote Canyon
#120  The Case of the Cosmic Kidnapping
#121  The Mystery in the Old Mine
#122  Carnival of Crime
#123  The Robot's Revenge
#124  Mystery with a Dangerous Beat
#125  Mystery on Makatunk Island
#126  Racing to Disaster
#127  Reel Thrills

## Available from MINSTREL Books

110

## *The* HARDY BOYS®

## THE SECRET OF SIGMA SEVEN

FRANKLIN W. DIXON

A MINSTREL® BOOK

PUBLISHED BY POCKET BOOKS

New York   London   Toronto   Sydney   Tokyo   Singapore

This book is a work of fiction. Names, characters, places and incidents are either the product of the author's imagination or are used fictitiously. Any resemblance to actual events or locales or persons, living or dead, is entirely coincidental.

A MINSTREL PAPERBACK *ORIGINAL*

 A Minstrel Book published by
POCKET BOOKS, a division of Simon & Schuster Inc.
1230 Avenue of the Americas, New York, NY 10020

Copyright © 1991 by Simon & Schuster Inc.
Cover artwork copyright © 1991 by Paul Bachem

Produced by Mega-Books of New York, Inc.

All rights reserved, including the right to reproduce this book or portions thereof in any form whatsoever. For information address Pocket Books, 1230 Avenue of the Americas, New York, NY 10020

ISBN: 0-671-72717-6

First Minstrel Books printing October 1991

10  9  8  7  6  5  4

THE HARDY BOYS MYSTERY STORIES is a trademark of Simon & Schuster Inc.

THE HARDY BOYS, A MINSTREL BOOK, and colophon are registered trademarks of Simon & Schuster Inc.

Printed in the U.S.A.

# Contents

1.  The Missing "Secret"                    1
2.  Eat Photons, Alien Dog!                12
3.  Elevator to Nowhere                    20
4.  If Cars Could Fly . . .                33
5.  The Huckster Room                      43
6.  Vanishing Act                          53
7.  Maker of Worlds                        63
8.  The Missing Master                     73
9.  Thunder and Lightning                  82
10. The Pressure Mounts                    93
11. A Meeting in the Woods                105
12. Fatal Surprise                        112
13. Invader from Mars                     119
14. The Magic Box                         126
15. Over the Edge                         132
16. Splash Landing                        144

# THE SECRET OF
# SIGMA SEVEN

# 1 The Missing "Secret"

"Take me to your leader, humanoids," the alien creature said in a muffled voice. "Or to an establishment where I can obtain some of the substance you Earthlings refer to as 'food.'"

Frank Hardy, a tall, muscular eighteen-year-old with dark hair and eyes, looked thoughtfully at the alien. It appeared to Frank to be a cross between a tall, hefty poodle puppy and a robot. Covered with damp, curly gray fur, it had glowing eyes that blinked alternately blue and red. On its head were a pair of floppy silver antennae that bounced back and forth every time it moved. It wore metallic three-fingered gloves on its front paws and clanking steel boots on its hind paws. As it stared at Frank and his

1

seventeen-year-old brother, Joe, it made a panting sound.

"I think it's an invader from the Planet of Wet Poodles," Frank said. "It's come to earth to lick us to death and keep us awake all night with its barking."

"I wouldn't worry about it," his brother said. Joe was slightly shorter than Frank and had light blond hair and blue eyes. "Whatever it is, it will probably fly back to its home planet soon. It can't breathe our Earth atmosphere. Too much oxygen."

"Come on, you guys," the alien said. "You know I'm supposed to be the Hairy Horror from Zepton." The creature reached up with a metallic paw and yanked its head straight off its shoulders. Underneath was the familiar round face of Chet Morton. Frank smiled at his friend, and Joe laughed out loud.

"Whew, it's hot under there!" Chet gasped. "I don't know how the guy who sold me this costume managed to breathe when he wore it."

"Maybe that's why he sold it to you," Joe suggested.

"You're not going to wear that at this convention all weekend, are you?" Frank asked.

"Nah," Chet said. "I'm wearing it tonight because it's the first night of the convention. And I'll wear it to the Cosmic Costume Contest tomorrow night. First prize is a trip to Florida to watch a space shuttle launch."

2

"Great," Joe said. "Maybe the shuttle will take you along. Then you can become a *real* space cadet."

"I hate to tell you this," Frank said, "but it looks as if you're going to have plenty of competition."

"You think so?" Chet said, frowning as he glanced around the room.

The three teenagers were standing in the crowded lobby of the Bayport Inn, a large, four-story motel on the outskirts of their hometown. The setting sun shone through the tall windows that formed one wall of the room. A bank of elevators was set into the opposite wall, and hallways branched off in two directions from the lobby. The room had a high, arching ceiling with exposed wooden beams, dark green leather couches and chairs, and a stone fireplace.

Brightly colored signs and posters, many of them featuring futuristic spacecraft and monsters from outer space, had been put up all over the lobby. Directly over Frank's head a cloth banner read Welcome to BayCon, Bayport's first science fiction convention! The Hardys and Chet watched as an assortment of strange creatures strolled through the lobby. Only a few feet away stood a young woman with large feathered wings growing straight out of her shoulder blades. One of her companions was a seven-foot-tall robot with metallic legs and arms. The other was a green, scaly creature with a long tail and a lizardlike snout who had a large bird perched on his shoulder. Other conventioneers were dressed

3

as purple-skinned barbarians and giant space-age insects.

"Just a typical day in the neighborhood," Frank commented. "If the neighborhood happens to be somewhere in the Andromeda Galaxy."

"This is really funny," Joe said, shaking his head. "I'm starting to feel like a weirdo dressed in my normal street clothes."

"Don't worry," said an unfamiliar voice from behind Frank's shoulder. "Some of these science fiction fans are almost normal underneath the costumes. Of course, the emphasis should be on the word *almost*."

Frank Hardy turned around to see a teenager with a friendly freckled face and short-cropped brown hair. The young man was three or four inches shorter than Frank and wore a yellow knit shirt and a pair of black jeans. Tucked under one arm was a large manila envelope.

"Hey, don't I know you?" Frank asked, eyeing the newcomer carefully. "Aren't you in one of my classes in school?"

"Right," the teenager said with a smile. "Brian Amchick. I moved to Bayport a few months ago. I'm in your trig class. First row on the right, second seat. You're Frank Hardy, aren't you?"

"That's me," Frank said. Then he added with a laugh, "You're the guy who always has the right answers to the questions and makes the rest of us look bad."

"I'll remember that," Brian said, chuckling. He turned to the others. "Are these your friends?"

4

"This is my brother, Joe. And the robot puppy from Alpha Centauri is our friend Chet Morton."

Chet raised one of his shiny paws. "Greetings from Zepton," he said in a deep voice. Joe rolled his eyes.

"Hi, guys," Brian said with a grin. "Nice to meet you. You just get here?"

"Yeah," Joe said. "We're still trying to figure out what's going on. Maybe you can show us around. This is our first sci-fi convention."

Brian winced. "Well, for starters, you'd better not refer to it as 'sci-fi.' Science fiction fans hate that term. We prefer to call it SF or just plain science fiction. And a convention is called a con."

"Uh, sorry," Joe said. "Guess I've got a lot to learn about sci-fi—er, science fiction."

"What do people do at a science fiction convention—I mean 'con'—anyway?" Frank asked. He pulled a booklet out of his pocket and showed it to Brian. "I looked at this program we got when we registered, but I can't figure out some of this stuff. It mentions a con party and a huckster room and something called filk singing."

Brian chuckled. "Mostly the con is a chance for science fiction fans—and, in a few cases, people who write SF books—to get together and have a good time."

"All right!" Joe exclaimed. "Sounds like my kind of place."

"There must be more to it than that, right?" Frank asked. "According to the program, there are scheduled events."

Brian nodded. "There'll be panels tomorrow and Sunday in the auditorium, where SF writers and experts will talk about science fiction." He patted the envelope he was carrying. "And if you're a collector of science fiction memorabilia like I am, you can pick up some great posters from old movies and back issues of SF magazines."

"We're not really collectors," Joe said.

"Of course," Brian went on, "there's the film tonight."

"Yeah," Joe said, his face brightening. "*The Secret of Sigma Seven!* The three of us have seen the first four films in the Galactic Saga series. We can't wait to see the new one."

"It's not every day that a major motion picture has its premiere in Bayport," Frank added. "We heard that the director, Simon Devoreaux, will be here in person to introduce it, and that he's giving a talk on his films."

"You heard right," Brian said. He glanced at his watch. "In fact, the movie should be starting in less than an hour."

"In that case," Chet said, "I think I'll head out to the van and change my clothes. If I don't get this costume off soon, I'll start to melt."

"Better hurry up," Joe called as Chet began to edge his way through the crowd milling around in the lobby. "We'll save you a seat—if we can."

Frank was about to ask Brian about one of the scheduled events when a loud, sharp voice suddenly cut through the noise of the crowd. "Feinbetter, you old phony! I knew you'd show up to try to convince the fans you know how to write. Why don't you give up writing and find an honest way to make a living?"

"Lay off, Hennessy," a second voice snapped.

"Who was that?" Frank asked Brian. "They sound like two guys looking for a fight."

"Oh, that's just Arlen Hennessy and Richard Feinbetter," Brian said. "They go through this routine at every con. Don't worry. They make a lot of noise, but they're really harmless."

The Hardys and Brian turned toward the crowd that had gathered in a semicircle at one corner of the lobby. A pair of men stood at the center of the crowd. One was a man of about sixty-five with thinning gray hair. He was wearing a plaid shirt and cotton pants too large for his thin frame. The other was a younger man who looked to be in his thirties. He had sharply cut facial features and tightly curled brown hair.

"How did you get in here, Hennessy?" the older man asked. "Did you walk in the front door or just ooze under it, like the slime you are?"

"Those two don't like each other much, do they?" Joe asked.

"Don't jump to conclusions," Brian said, a sly smile on his face. "It's just an act. SF fans have come to expect Feinbetter and Hennessy to be at each other's throats, so they have to live up to expectations. Later tonight they'll be at the con party like everybody else, having a great time."

7

Frank glanced at the two men as they continued their argument. "Are they both writers?"

"Yeah," Brian said. He gestured toward the older man. "Feinbetter's an old pro, one of the last writers from the so-called Golden Age of Science Fiction. Used to write for *Astounding Science Fiction* magazine. He's the guest of honor at this convention."

"What about the other guy?" Frank asked. "Arlen Hennessy?"

"He's one of the hottest writers in the field right now," Brian said. "He's won a lot of awards for his stories, and he's only about half Feinbetter's age. He's got a big mouth that's been known to get him in some trouble."

"Sounds as if they both have big mouths," Frank said. He watched for a moment as Hennessy and Feinbetter exchanged another round of insults and the fans surrounding them laughed.

"What about this movie?" Joe asked. "Maybe we'd better start looking for seats."

"Good idea," Brian said. "Follow me." He led them to the rear of the lobby and down a hallway, then through a door marked Conference Room A. "This is where the film will be shown," he said.

Joe looked over the rows of folding chairs that had been set up in the large room. About half of the seats were already filled, and a crowd of people continued to pour in through the doors. Frank, Joe, and Brian found a row of seats about midway back and grabbed four of them.

Frank settled in his chair and looked around the

8

room. A wide screen had been set up in front. In the center aisle sat a pair of large movie projectors on carts. Next to the screen was a colorful poster with the title *The Secret of Sigma Seven* written across it in bright red letters. Beneath the title was a picture of a long-haired, muscular young man dressed in black armor. In the background were stars, spaceships, and brightly colored explosions.

"I can't wait to see this movie," Joe said, sitting next to his brother. "The last one in the series, *Warriors from the Forgotten Star,* had incredible special effects, and I heard that the effects in this one are even better."

"Did I miss anything?" Chet asked as he slid into the chair next to Joe. He was holding a huge bag of popcorn, which he offered to his friends.

"You're just in time," Frank said as he took a handful of popcorn and motioned toward the screen.

In front of the screen a dark-haired woman who looked to be in her mid-twenties was setting up a microphone. She tapped on the mike a couple of times, then spoke into it, causing the speakers on the wall behind her to emit a high-pitched whining noise. After she adjusted the microphone, she cleared her throat and began talking.

"I, um, would like to welcome all of you to BayCon and to our special showing of Simon Devoreaux's new film, *The Secret of Sigma Seven,*" she said nervously, glancing sideways to a door on the left.

There was a burst of applause and whistling at the mention of the film's title. When the crowd quieted

9

down, the young woman adjusted her eyeglasses and continued speaking.

"I'm Linda Klein, the convention chairwoman and president of the Bayport Science Fiction Society, or BSFS, as we like to call ourselves," the young woman said, pronouncing the name of the society as "bissfiss."

"We're really excited about the premiere of this film," she went on. "Because science fiction fans have liked his Galactic Saga films so much, Mr. Devoreaux felt it would be appropriate to premiere the latest movie in the saga at a science fiction convention. We're really proud that he chose BayCon for this momentous event."

She looked at her watch, then glanced at the door again. "Er, maybe you'd like to hear a little about the history of BSFS before we show the movie."

"We want to see the movie!" somebody in the audience shouted.

"Well, we're not quite ready yet," the young woman continued. "Mr. Devoreaux was supposed to be here by now and was going to introduce the film himself, but I'm afraid that he—"

Her glance suddenly shifted to the door of the room. Frank turned and followed her gaze. A tanned and handsome middle-aged man with platinum hair and a commanding manner strode down the center aisle, accompanied by a small entourage of men in suits. Frank recognized Simon Devoreaux immediately from pictures he'd seen in magazines. The two large men walking close to him looked like body-

10

guards, while the others trailing along behind were probably private secretaries or studio executives. One of them, a tall, ruddy-faced man with a mustache and curly reddish hair, looked slightly familiar to Frank. Devoreaux walked up to the microphone and stood next to Linda Klein.

"Mr. Devoreaux!" the young woman exclaimed. "It's . . . it's great to see you. We're all ready to see your new film."

The audience began to applaud as Devoreaux stepped up to the microphone. Linda Klein moved off to one side of the movie screen. Frank noticed the angry expression on Devoreaux's face as he began to speak.

"I'm afraid there's not going to be a film tonight," the movie director announced in a deep, clear voice.

"No film?" somebody in the audience called out. "I passed up a trip to Florida to be here!"

Devoreaux shrugged. "Well, there's no way anyone's going to see this film tonight—or anytime soon."

"Why not?" someone asked.

"Because there *is* no film!" Devoreaux exclaimed. *"The Secret of Sigma Seven* has vanished, disappeared. In short, the movie has been stolen!"

# 2 Eat Photons, Alien Dog!

"Stolen?" Frank jumped to his feet. "How did that happen?"

"We took every precaution against theft—or thought we had," Devoreaux replied. "But some crook got to the film, anyway. One of my assistants—a former assistant, I should say— stupidly left it inside my limousine. When we entered the motel, the assistant realized he had forgotten to bring the film. I rushed back to the parking lot myself to get it, but it was gone. Someone had taken it out of the limousine."

"I want my money back!" somebody shouted. "I paid good money to get into this convention, and it sure wasn't to hang around with all these freaks in weird costumes."

"That's not my problem," Devoreaux said curtly. "You should talk with the people who put on this so-called convention. I have only one more thing to say," he added, glaring at the audience. "If the person who stole the print of my film is in this audience now, I want you to know that the studio will prosecute you to the full extent of the law when you are captured—unless you return the film this weekend, in perfect condition. And if any bootleg copies of the film should be made, I'll also prosecute anyone caught distributing them. Is that clear?"

Apparently, it was clear enough, Frank thought, because nobody asked any questions. Devoreaux stepped away from the microphone, exchanged a few words with the members of his entourage, then began walking toward the door.

After the director had left the room, Linda Klein moved back to the microphone and said a few apologetic words, but no one in the audience paid attention to her. Everyone was too busy talking excitedly about the stolen film.

"This is awful," Chet moaned, a disappointed look on his face. "I've been looking forward to this movie all week."

Frank leaned back in his chair and frowned. "You know, I'd be angry, too, if somebody stole something that had taken me a whole year's work. But Devoreaux doesn't seem too concerned about his fans. I mean, the least he could have done was to say he was sorry for the inconvenience."

"I don't believe this whole thing," Chet said.

"Who'd steal a copy of a movie? What are they going to do with it, anyway?"

"That's not hard to figure out," Joe said. "They're probably going to sell it."

"But who'd buy it?" Brian asked. "Only somebody who owns one of those big projectors"—he gestured toward the oversize movie projectors in the middle of the aisle—"would be able to watch it."

"Not if they transferred it to videocassette first," Frank said. "Just about everybody's got a VCR."

Joe snapped his fingers. "Right! Bootleg videotapes, like Devoreaux said. I read an article about that the other day. There's a big black market for videotapes of new movies. Especially movies that haven't even been released yet, like this one."

"And I bet there are a lot of people who'd pay good money to get a videotape of the latest movie from Simon Devoreaux," Frank said.

"*I* sure would," Chet joked. Leaning forward in his seat to face the others, he whispered, "Where can I find the guy who'll sell me a copy?"

Grabbing a handful of the popcorn from the bag Chet held, Joe said, "Unless you want to go to jail, I think you'd better wait until this one hits the theaters here in Bayport. Anyway, Devoreaux must have a master print of this film back in Hollywood, so he can turn out more copies."

"But who in this crowd would have the equipment to transfer a film to video?" Frank asked. "That's not the kind of thing the average person might own."

14

"The average person doesn't dress like a zombie from Zepton," Joe quipped, looking around the room at the rapidly departing crowd. "But most of these people probably wouldn't know what to do with the film if they had it, so they aren't suspects in the crime."

"Suspects?" Brian asked, wrinkling his brow. "You guys really are detectives, aren't you? I've heard that you've helped the police investigate a few crimes around the Bayport area."

"We like to pitch in from time to time," Frank said. "Our father's a private investigator, and he's taught us about detective work."

"So are you going to help Simon Devoreaux get his movie back?" Brian asked.

"We'll help him if he asks us," Joe replied.

Frank glanced toward the door. Devoreaux was standing outside the room, talking to Linda Klein. The young woman looked upset. The movie director still wore an angry expression on his face. "From the looks of him," Frank said, "he doesn't seem like the type who would ask us. Maybe we'd better leave this case to the Bayport police."

Chet stood up. "Well, if we're not going to see the film," he said dejectedly, "let's go get something to eat."

"Not a bad idea," Frank said. "Want to go over to Mr. Pizza with us, Brian? We can come back here later."

"Sounds great," Brian said. "Let's go."

As the four teenagers left the room, they saw Simon Devoreaux and his entourage heading down the crowded hallway. Linda Klein trailed along after the director's group.

"Please, Mr. Devoreaux," Frank heard her plead, "I wish you would reconsider your decision not to give your talk. We'd all like to hear what you have to say." But the director ignored her and continued to stride down the hallway toward the lobby.

"Poor Linda," Brian said with a sigh. "She really worked hard organizing this con. And Devoreaux was supposed to be the main attraction."

"He's the main attraction, all right," Joe said.

The chattering crowd in the lobby had fallen silent. Everyone stared at the director as he loudly ordered one of the men in his entourage to call his lawyers.

Just then the Hardys saw Brian look across the lobby, an expression of surprise on his face. They saw their friend was looking at a short, balding man in his late thirties. The man was standing inside the front entrance of the motel.

"I can't believe it," Brian said, hurrying over to the man. The Hardys and Chet followed their friend.

"Uncle Pete!" Brian exclaimed. "What are you doing here? I thought you were up in Massachusetts."

The man smiled at Brian in a distracted way, as though he had something else on his mind. Frank could see the family resemblance between Brian and

16

his uncle. Brian's uncle had the same round face and friendly expression as his nephew.

"Oh, Brian," the man said. "Good to see you. Wondered if I'd run into you here."

"Hey, guys," Brian said, turning to the others. "This is my uncle Pete. Pete Amchick. He's a professor up at Boston Tech. Uncle Pete, meet Frank, Joe, and Chet, friends of mine."

Pete Amchick shook hands with the teens, but Frank got the impression that he barely noticed them. Brian's uncle was busy surveying the crowd in the lobby.

"I'm hoping to talk to Simon Devoreaux," Pete said. "But I need to talk to him alone."

"Boy, did you pick the wrong night," Joe said with a laugh. "I don't think Devoreaux's in the mood to speak to anybody right now."

"Oh, I think he'll want to talk to me," Pete Amchick said, smiling slightly. "We have some things to discuss."

"Well, here's your chance," Chet told him. "Devoreaux's coming toward us."

The Hardys turned to follow Chet's gaze. Devoreaux and his entourage were heading toward the door. The two large bodyguards kept the crowd out of his path as Devoreaux made his way through the lobby.

"Excuse me," Pete Amchick said, stepping up to the director. "Mr. Devoreaux? Could I speak with you for a moment?"

17

The silver-haired film director paid no attention to Pete Amchick. Instead, he turned to a young man in his group and said in his deep voice, "I left my briefcase in my room. Get it for me, would you?" The young man nodded and hurried off.

"Come on, Uncle Pete," Brian said, taking his uncle's arm. "Let's go grab some dinner."

But Pete Amchick pulled away from his nephew. "Not now, Brian. I need to talk to Devoreaux," Pete said urgently. "It's very important." He started to approach the director again, but before he could say anything, Linda Klein walked up to Devoreaux.

"Mr. Devoreaux, I've notified the police about the theft," she said. "Once again, please accept my apologies for this terrible occurrence."

The director looked at her, a stony expression on his face. "Apologies won't get my film back, Ms. Klein," he said. "If the film isn't returned shortly, you and the Bayport Inn will be hearing from my lawyers."

Frank noticed that Linda looked very unhappy to hear this from the director.

"Eat photons, alien dog!" a voice suddenly shouted.

Devoreaux froze in his tracks and stared toward the door in disbelief. Frank turned to see a person dressed like the hero of *The Secret of Sigma Seven* standing by the door. He wore black armor and a helmet that formed a mask over his face. His long black cape almost touched the floor.

18

Smiling maliciously, the armor-clad man pulled a zap gun out of his holster and pointed it directly at Devoreaux, who was stunned.

The man in black pulled the trigger on the gun. There was an exploding sound, and a bullet sped out of the muzzle directly at the startled director!

# 3 Elevator to Nowhere

Devoreaux jumped aside at the last second as the bullet whizzed past his shoulder, blasting a two-inch hole in the wall behind him. The echo of the gunshot reverberated through the crowded lobby for several seconds as all heads turned toward the person in black armor.

Frank Hardy rushed forward, grabbed the arm of the man who had fired the shot, and yanked the gun from his hand. To his surprise, the assailant put up no resistance whatsoever. He simply pulled off his helmet and mask, revealing that he was not much older than fourteen.

"Let me at him!" one of Devoreaux's bodyguards exclaimed as he rushed forward and grasped the teenager's other arm. Frank stepped back and let the

20

bodyguard take charge of the young man. He handed the gun to the second bodyguard.

Frank studied Devoreaux's assailant carefully. He looked tall for his age. He had pale skin and blond hair that had been messed up when he had pulled off the helmet. Frank guessed that he was as startled by the gunshot as everyone else in the room.

"That was a close one," Joe said, stepping beside his brother. "You did a great job getting the gun away from that guy."

"He didn't put up much of a fight," Frank said with a shrug. "There's something funny going on here."

"Hilarious," Chet said. "When the bullets stop flying, maybe I'll be able to laugh."

Simon Devoreaux walked up to his assailant. By now the bodyguard was pinning the young man's arms tightly behind his back. "Who are you? Why did you try to kill me?" Devoreaux demanded. His voice was angry, but Frank noticed that he sounded quite shaken as well. "Are you the person who stole the film?"

"M-my name is F-Fred," the teenager stammered. "Fred Johnson. And I—I didn't try to kill you. I didn't even know that thing was l-l-loaded! Somebody handed it to me and said I should shoot it at you as a joke. I thought it was just a toy gun."

As the second bodyguard cracked open the gun, Frank saw for the first time that it was only a toy zap gun. But Frank was amazed to see that inside the plastic shell of the zap gun was a small pistol. Its

21

trigger was wired to the trigger of the zap gun, so that when the toy gun was fired, the real pistol fired, too.

"Here's what he tried to shoot you with," the bodyguard said. "Somebody went to a lot of trouble to hide this pistol inside the plastic gun."

Devoreaux glanced at the pistol, then turned back to the frightened Fred Johnson. "Who gave you the gun? Is he in this room now?"

"He was here a second ago," Fred replied, looking desperately around the lobby. "He was standing over there. B-but I don't see him now. He must have left."

"What did he look like?" Frank asked. "Would you recognize him if you saw him again?"

"He—he was wearing a costume," Fred Johnson stammered. "Like one of those porcupine creatures from your films, Mr. Devoreaux."

"Great," Joe muttered. "There are hundreds of people in costume at this convention. I've seen five giant porcupines in the last ten minutes."

Devoreaux turned to the bodyguard who held Fred Johnson. "Hold on to this young man until the police arrive. I'm sure they'll have a few questions for him."

"I can't tell you how sorry I am for this incident," Linda Klein said to the director. "I can't imagine how it could have happened. The planning committee made a serious attempt to restrict the use of toy weapons at the convention."

But instead of replying, Devoreaux just motioned to his entourage to follow him out the door.

Linda Klein stood looking after him, a worried expression on her face.

"Maybe we should help her out," Frank said, gesturing toward the young woman. "She's probably going to be in a lot of trouble if nobody finds out who stole Devoreaux's film."

"Not to mention finding whoever gave Fred Johnson that gun," Joe said. "The kid doesn't sound like a liar or a criminal. It looks to me like somebody was using him to get at Devoreaux."

Frank told Brian and Chet that he and Joe would see them later. Then the Hardys walked over to Linda Klein.

"Excuse me," Frank said. "We were wondering if we could give you a hand with this incident, maybe help you find the guy who took Mr. Devoreaux's film."

"What?" Linda Klein stared at Frank, a baffled look on her face. "Who are you?"

"I'm Frank Hardy, and this is my brother Joe. We've had some experience with detective work."

"Oh, yes," Linda Klein said, a look of comprehension coming over her face. "I've heard of you guys. I don't know what you can do about this, though. Simon Devoreaux is already planning to sue the BSFS for the loss of the *Sigma Seven* reels and the damage to his reputation. And there's no telling what he's going to do about what just happened." Frank saw that Linda was growing more agitated. "It may take years for the BSFS to pay for this," she continued. "The other members will never forgive me!"

23

"Maybe we can help out," Joe said. "If the guy who stole the film is still in the motel, we might be able to find him, and that may persuade Simon Devoreaux not to sue you after all."

A hopeful glimmer appeared in Linda Klein's eyes. "You think there's a chance? What about that kid who tried to shoot Devoreaux with the toy gun? Do you think he might be behind the theft, too?"

"I doubt it," Frank said. "I think he was telling the truth when he said that someone gave him the gun."

"But that probably means that the person who stole the film is still here—or was a few minutes ago," Joe added. "Assuming that whoever stole the film also gave the gun to the kid. So maybe there's still a chance we can catch him."

"All right," Linda said. "I'd really appreciate it if you could help. I'm sure I can clear it with the convention committee. I'll be talking to the police in a few minutes, but we'll still need all the assistance we can get. Thanks a lot!"

"You can thank us when we catch the thief," Frank said with a grin.

"Maybe you can help *us* out," Joe said. "Do you know anybody who dislikes Devoreaux enough to steal his film—or kill him?"

Linda shrugged. "Nobody in the club knows Devoreaux at all, except by reputation. If he has enemies, they're probably out in Hollywood, not here."

"One of them *must* be here," Frank said. "Since this is where the film was stolen."

"I wish I could give you more help," Linda said with an apologetic smile. "Listen, I overheard Devoreaux say he was having a meeting with his special-effects director at the Shore Restaurant. I'm going to call the restaurant and tell Devoreaux that I've got a pair of well-known private detectives on the case. Maybe that will change his attitude." She turned and vanished into the crowd again. Frank and Joe looked at each other.

"Well?" Joe said. "Now that we've promised to solve this case, what do we do next?"

"We could start out by questioning the kid with the gun," Frank suggested.

"Not a bad idea," Joe said. "Let's go."

Devoreaux's bodyguard was still holding the costumed teenager with his arms pinned behind his back, waiting for the police to arrive. Frank gently nudged aside several curious bystanders as he and Joe came up beside the frightened-looking young man.

"Excuse me," Frank said to the bodyguard. "Do you mind if we ask this guy a few questions?"

The bodyguard, a hulking man with wide shoulders and a neck as thick as a tree trunk, looked at the Hardys with narrowed eyes. "You're not the police."

"No, we're not," Joe said. "We're working for the people who put on this convention, and we'd like to find out a few things from this kid."

"I guess it can't hurt," the bodyguard said with a shrug. "But I'll be right here, okay?"

"Sure thing," Frank said, turning to Fred Johnson.

"Your name's Fred, right? I'm Frank Hardy. You said a minute ago that somebody gave you that gun?"

"Yeah," said the boy, still trembling. "I didn't mean to shoot Mr. Devoreaux. Honest!"

"We believe you," Joe said. "We were just wondering if you noticed anything unusual about the guy who handed you the gun. Besides the fact that he was dressed as a porcupine," he added with a slight smirk.

Fred Johnson thought about it for a moment, then shook his head "N-no," he said. "That's all. He had on this costume and— Wait a minute! There *was* something else. He had on this . . . this medallion around his neck, outside the costume."

"What did the medallion look like?" Frank asked.

"It was green," the teenager said promptly. "Kind of like jade. And round. There was something carved in it, too."

"What was the carving?" Frank asked.

"A crescent moon and a star," Fred replied.

Joe looked at his brother. "That's something to go on, at least."

Just then the Hardys spotted a pair of uniformed police officers entering the lobby. The bodyguard nodded at them. The officers took hold of Fred and led him out of the motel.

"Hey, you guys, I thought we were going over to Mr. Pizza," Chet said as he and Brian walked up to the Hardys. "I'm starved."

"Me, too," Joe said. "Let's head out."

"I've got a better idea," Brian said, motioning toward the nearest wall. "See that poster? Somebody put it up while you were talking to that kid."

Frank looked at the poster and read out loud. "'Because of the unfortunate cancellation of this evening's presentation of *The Secret of Sigma Seven,* the con party will begin at 9 P.M.'"

"The con party?" Chet asked. "That's the party mentioned in the schedule, isn't it?"

Brian nodded. "It's the official party of the convention," he explained. "Lots of food and sodas, all free."

"This is definitely my kind of convention," Chet said with delight. "I should have started coming to these things years ago."

"I knew Chet was a serious science fiction fan," Frank said, grinning.

"By the way, Brian," Joe said, "what happened to your uncle?"

"He followed Devoreaux when he left," Brian said. "Kept saying that he really had to talk to him."

"Do you have any idea why your uncle is so desperate to talk to Devoreaux?" Frank asked Brian.

Brian shook his head. "Uncle Pete isn't very talkative. And tonight he's being even more quiet."

"Come on," Joe said. "Let's get to the party. Do you know the way, Brian?"

"Sure," Brian said. "It's on the fourth floor. Follow me."

He led them to the main elevators at the back of

the lobby. When the doors opened on the fourth floor, Frank could hear the sounds of a party in the distance. He and the others followed Brian to a large suite.

Inside the suite, which consisted of several interconnected rooms, Frank could see people of all ages standing around talking and eating. Frank also spotted the tall, ruddy-faced, red-haired man he'd seen with Devoreaux earlier that evening. The man was talking in an animated tone to a young woman. Frank overheard the man say that he had arrived in Bayport that afternoon and had liked the town very much.

"Who *is* that guy?" Frank muttered to himself. "I know I've seen him before tonight."

"I'm headed over there," Chet said, pointing across the main room at a long table filled with sandwiches and sodas. "Free food, here I come!"

"Let's grab some eats and see if anybody in this room's wearing a medallion like the one Fred Johnson described," Joe suggested.

"I see some people I want to talk to," Brian said. "I'll catch up with you guys later."

The Hardys joined Chet at the end of the buffet line. As they moved down the line, they heard laughter coming from one corner of the room. Frank looked over and saw a group of fans clustered around Richard Feinbetter, the gray-haired science fiction writer they had seen in the lobby earlier.

After they had gotten their sandwiches and sodas, the Hardys and Chet walked over to listen to what

28

the writer had to say. Feinbetter had just finished telling the group a humorous story about his early years as a writer. He was smiling and seemed to be having a great time. Then someone in the crowd said the name Simon Devoreaux.

"Devoreaux?" Feinbetter snapped in a raspy voice. "That phony? He's never had an original idea in his life. He's just a hack moviemaker. That kind of guy gives science fiction a bad name."

Raising his eyebrows, Joe glanced at Frank, then back at Feinbetter. Could the writer have had a reason to swipe Devoreaux's movie?

"It's too bad about that film being stolen, Mr. Feinbetter," Joe said casually.

"Too bad?" Feinbetter said, looking Joe up and down. "It's the best thing that could have happened. Devoreaux got what was coming to him."

Frank studied Feinbetter closely. "What do you mean by that? Sounds as if you don't like Simon Devoreaux very much."

Feinbetter started to reply, then seemed to think better of it. "Never mind," he said. "I shouldn't have said what I just did about Devoreaux. I don't want to give anybody the idea that I approve of stealing property."

"*Do* you approve of stealing property?" Joe pressed.

"And what kind of question is that, young man?" Feinbetter said sharply. "We taught better manners to young people in *my* day."

29

"If you think my brother's manners are bad here, you should see him at the dinner table," Frank said with a grin.

Joe shot Frank a dirty look as Feinbetter went back to telling stories. The Hardys listened for a moment, then wandered away.

"We may have found our first suspect," Joe said.

"Yeah," Frank said. "Unless my instincts are off, I think Richard Feinbetter has something against Devoreaux."

"But does he dislike him enough to steal his film?" Joe asked.

"Or to try and kill him?" Frank added. "Maybe we should see what we can turn up on Feinbetter."

"In the meantime," Joe said, "let's split up and look around the party for anything else that might be a lead."

"I'll check back with you in a half hour," Frank said.

The elder Hardy wandered around the room and struck up conversations with several fans but learned nothing significant. The stolen film seemed to be the big topic of conversation, but nobody knew any more about it than Frank already did. And he didn't spot anyone wearing a green medallion. Finally he located his brother.

"I came up empty, too," Joe reported. "Let's call it a night."

They found Chet chatting with a girl who was wheeling out food from the kitchen and Brian talking with a group of fans. The Hardys explained the situation to their friends.

"Sorry you didn't have better luck, guys," Brian said. "I'll walk with you and Chet back down to the lobby."

As they left the room, Frank spotted a lone fan standing next to a door at the end of a dimly lit hallway. The tall fan wore a NASA-style space suit, complete with oxygen tanks strapped to his back. He gestured at the four teens and said something unintelligible through the face mask of his helmet. It was impossible to make out any details of his face through the clouded glass.

"Hey, guys," the fan said in a muffled voice. "You need to get downstairs? There's an elevator right here."

"What?" Joe said. "I thought the elevators were in the middle of the building, over the lobby."

"So did I," Brian said. "Well, you learn something new every day."

Joe looked at the door next to the space-suited fan. Sure enough, it was an elevator door. As they watched, the man reached over and, with a gloved hand, pressed the button marked down. The light over the door blinked on.

Frank studied the space-suited fan. Even though there were a lot of people at the convention in costumes, there was something about this fan that wasn't quite right. But Frank couldn't put his finger on it.

31

The elevator door slid open. Joe moved forward.

Wait a minute, Frank thought. I've got it. That guy's wearing a green medallion around his neck.

He turned to stop his brother from getting on the elevator.

It was too late. Joe stepped through the doorway and gasped. There was no elevator car on the other side of the door. With a sinking feeling in the pit of his stomach, Joe realized that he was stepping into wide open space.

And the ground was four stories below!

# 4 If Cars Could Fly . . .

Joe began whirling his arms wildly to keep his balance. One of his feet was already pointing out into space, and the other was barely staying in contact with the floor behind him.

Just as Joe was about to fall forward into a four-story plunge, Frank grabbed him around the waist and pulled him backward.

Joe tumbled to the floor with a loud gasp. "Whew! That was a close one!"

Frank spun around to confront the man in the space suit, but he was nowhere to be seen.

"Which way did the guy in the space suit go?" Frank asked.

"I think he ran to the right," Brian said, pointing

33

toward the far end of the hallway. "He looked like he was in a hurry."

"I bet he was," Frank said, racing down the hallway. When he reached the end, he looked to the hall to the right and saw that it was lined with doors on both sides. A bright red exit light gleamed at the end of the corridor.

Great, Frank thought. He could have gone through the exit or ducked into any one of these rooms.

Discouraged, Frank returned to his companions at the other end of the hall.

"This is really weird," Chet said, examining the elevator. "It's out of order. I can barely make out the ground floor in the dark, but it looks like a long way down. The elevator car must be down at the bottom."

"I wish somebody'd told me that before I tried to take a ride in the thing," Joe said as he got to his feet.

Moving to Chet's side, Frank took his penlight and shined it inside the shaft. He saw that two wires were connected to the terminals of the elevator button on the other side of the wall. The wires led upward to a motor that controlled the doors.

"Look at this," Frank said. "That guy must have rigged the button to open the doors. Usually the button just signals the car to move up or down."

"Right," Joe said, looking into the shaft. "And usually the doors open when the car stops on a floor. But why did the light go on when that guy pressed the down button?"

"Well, it looks as if the light and the door were

34

wired on the same circuit," Frank replied. "That guy did a good job of fooling us."

Chet squinted into the darkness. "I guess the motel is repairing this elevator."

"Hey," Joe said, kneeling down. "This looks like the remains of a wooden barrier." He reached into the hole and pulled out a piece of cardboard that had been wedged behind a beam. "And here's a sign that was supposed to warn people away."

"It would have warned *us* away," Frank said, "if our astronaut hadn't hidden it."

"So why do you think this guy wanted to kill you?" Chet asked Joe.

"He must have found out somehow that we're investigating the theft of Devoreaux's film," Joe answered. "What I want to know is whether or not this is the same guy who engineered the attack on Devoreaux."

"I think I can answer that one," Frank said. "Didn't you notice what he had around his neck?"

"Oh, no," Joe said. "Not the green medallion."

"You got it," Frank said. "With the moon and star."

"So he could be the same guy who gave the gun to that kid in the lobby!" Joe exclaimed.

"Right," Frank said. "If we'd noticed sooner, we could have nabbed him."

"You two should be careful," Brian said. "Not only is someone after Devoreaux, but now he's after you, too."

"Don't worry," Joe said. "If we run into anybody

35

wearing a green medallion again, I'm going to jump him first and ask questions later."

"We can ask around the party and see if anybody knows the guy in the space suit," Frank said. "But first we'd better call hotel maintenance and have them do something about this elevator."

Frank called down to the lobby from the phone in the party suite. Two hotel staffers arrived ten minutes later, expressing amazement that somebody would have removed the protective barriers and the sign intended to prevent anyone from going near the broken elevator. They explained that it was a freight elevator, used only by employees.

The Hardys spent another half hour at the party, but nobody admitted to having seen the man in the space suit. Finally, with Brian and Chet in tow, the Hardys returned to the lobby, where they said goodbye to Brian. Then they drove home, dropping Chet off at the Morton farm on the way.

"Hey," Frank said to his brother. "Is that car floating in the air?"

It was the morning after the con party. Frank was steering the Hardys' converted police van into the parking lot of the Bayport Inn. About fifty feet away, along the curved access lane that led up to the front door of the motel, a sleek white vehicle that looked a little like a futuristic sports car with a convertible top was pulled over to the curb. It seemed to be hovering about two feet off the ground. In the front seat sat a tall, cheerful-looking man in his late thirties, with a ruddy complexion, a reddish mustache, and curly hair.

"Huh?" Joe said, seated next to Frank in the front of the van. He squinted in the direction of the floating car. "Yeah," he said at last. "I think you're right. Now I've seen everything."

"Thank goodness," Frank said. "I thought maybe I'd finally gone bonkers."

"That's still a possibility," Chet said. He was kneeling in the back behind Joe's seat, looking out the window over his friend's shoulder. "But that really is a floating car."

"I recognize that guy in the driver's seat," Frank said. "He was with Devoreaux last night, and I saw him at the con party. I've been trying to remember where I've seen him before."

Frank pulled the van into an empty space, and the three teens got out. The first thing they saw was a large green canvas tent that had been erected in the middle of the parking lot. Frank studied the tent for a moment, then joined his brother and Chet at the front door of the motel. The car they had noticed on the way in was still floating just where they had last seen it, and a small crowd had gathered around it. As he got closer, Frank could hear the car make a loud hissing noise, like air escaping from a balloon.

"You know," Frank said, wrinkling his brow, "that looks similar to one of the cars the bad guys were driving in *The Cosmic Maelstrom*, the second movie in the Galactic Saga series."

"Yeah," Chet said, his face lighting up. "The ones

they used in that chase scene on the Planet of Glass. Remember when those two guys chased each other right off the edge of a cliff in their flying cars?"

"Wait a minute," Joe said suddenly. "I know why that guy in the car looks familiar. I saw his picture in a magazine article about Simon Devoreaux."

"Hey, you're right," Frank said. "I read that article, too. That's what's-his-name, Jack Gillis, the guy who does all the special effects for Devoreaux's movies."

"This looks interesting," Joe said. "I'd like to talk to him."

When they reached Gillis, Frank could see that the special-effects director enjoyed talking to his admirers. He was leaning over the side of the open-topped vehicle, chatting amiably with the crowd. Fans shot questions at him, and he freely shot back answers.

"Did you use this very car in the Galactic Saga movies?" a teenage girl with long black hair asked.

"You bet," Gillis said. "We used it in the last two movies. It cost a lot to build it, so we wanted to get as much mileage out of it as we could."

"I thought you used miniature models in your films," a balding man in a plaid shirt asked. "Not full-size vehicles like this one."

"We usually do," Gillis replied. "I've built a lot of those models myself—spaceships, mostly. But it's easier to film people sitting in one of these hovercars if you've got a full-size vehicle for them to sit in. We can't shrink the people down to the size of the model."

"What keeps this car up in the air?" Frank asked. "Some kind of air jets?"

"Sort of," Gillis replied. "There's an engine inside that drives several high-speed fans to create a cushion of compressed air underneath the car."

"Wow," Chet said in awe. "Where can I buy one of these hovercars?"

Gillis laughed. "I'm afraid you can't. There are only a few in existence. Anyway, you wouldn't want to drive around in one. They can hold only two people at a time, and everything else has to be stripped to the bone. Put any luggage in this thing, and it would sink right back to the ground. It really can't carry much weight. And the noise from these high-speed fans would start driving you crazy after a while."

"I don't care," Chet said. "I want one anyway. You guys could get rich marketing these things."

"We're already rich," Gillis boasted with a chuckle. "Anyway, I've got to get moving now. We're setting up an exhibit of props and costumes from the Galactic Saga movies in the parking lot, inside that large tent over there." He waved his hand toward the tent. "I hope you'll drop by this afternoon to get another look at this car—and a few other things, too."

"We'll be there," Frank said as Gillis drove away in the hovercar.

39

"That was neat," Joe said. "We may have missed the film last night, but there's still a lot of stuff to do around here."

"Like catch a criminal?" Frank suggested.

"Yeah, that, too," Joe said.

Frank opened the glass front doors and entered the lobby a few steps ahead of his brother and Chet. Science fiction fans were milling back and forth, and even more of them were wearing costumes than the night before, Frank noticed. Then he remembered that the costume party was scheduled for that evening.

"I guess you guys are going to look for the film thief, right?" Chet asked.

Frank nodded. "And I have a feeling we've got a long day ahead of us."

"Then I'm going to go scout out this convention," Chet said. "If I see or hear anything suspicious, I'll let you know."

"Okay," Joe said. "Why don't you meet us in the lobby around lunchtime?"

"Right," Chet said. "See you around."

"So what do you think we should do now?" Joe asked his brother after Chet had left.

"Our only clue so far," Frank said, "is what we heard Feinbetter say last night. So maybe we'd better see if we can find out a few things about him."

"Good idea," Joe said. "And maybe we can figure out if there's any place around here where the thief could sell stolen videotapes."

"Brian can probably give us the story on that,"

Frank said. "He seems to know his way around this convention. I wonder where he is this morning."

Joe pointed to a large group of people in a corner of the room. "There's another crowd," he said to Frank. "What's going on this time?"

Frank craned his neck. "Looks like that young writer Brian pointed out to us yesterday," Frank said. "What was his name? Arlen Hennessy?"

"Oh, right," Joe said. "Isn't he supposed to be a friend of Feinbetter's? Maybe he could tell us a thing or two about the guy."

"Couldn't hurt to ask," Frank said. He and Joe pushed their way into the crowd, trying to get close enough to hear Hennessy talk.

Hennessy appeared to be having a good time. He was a compactly built man, wearing an expensive sweater and tight-fitting pants. He was good-looking, with piercing green eyes, tightly curled hair, and a rapid-fire style of speaking—sort of like a stand-up comedian, Frank thought.

"The Galactic Saga movies?" Hennessy was saying in response to something one of the fans had said. "You actually *like* that trash? My next-door neighbor makes better home movies of his kid's birthday parties than anything Simon Devoreaux has ever directed."

"But, Arlen," a young male fan at the front of the crowd said, "the first movie in the saga won the Orbit Award as best science fiction movie of the year. I know *I* voted for it."

"How much did Simon Devoreaux pay you for

41

your vote?" Hennessy said, a wicked gleam in his eye. "Has your taste in movies always been that bad?"

"You don't like Devoreaux's films very much, do you, Arlen?" somebody asked.

Hennessy struck a pose of mock innocence. "Did I say that? Surely you must have misinterpreted my words. I don't dislike Devoreaux's films. I *despise* them."

"I stand corrected," the fan said, grinning.

Joe looked at Frank and whispered, "This guy doesn't like Devoreaux any more than Feinbetter does. Maybe he's the one who tried to shoot him."

Frank nodded. "We should check Hennessy out, too," he whispered back.

"Hey, Arlen," Joe said, assuming the familiar tone of voice that the other fans were using. "You wouldn't happen to know who stole Simon Devoreaux's movie, would you?"

"A-ha!" Hennessy said, raising his hands in front of him in a theatrical gesture to quiet the crowd. "Somebody wants to know who stole Simon Devoreaux's film? No problem! I know who stole the film—and you can quote me on this."

He leaned forward and said in a loud stage whisper, "It was Feinbetter. My old buddy Richard Feinbetter stole Simon Devoreaux's film."

# 5 The Huckster Room

Frank and Joe edged their way through the crowd until they were right in front of Arlen Hennessy.

"Are you saying you know who committed the crime?" Frank asked the writer. When Hennessy smiled smugly and nodded, Frank continued. "Then why haven't you told the police?"

"That's aiding and abetting a felony," Joe added. "You'd better tell us everything you know about Richard Feinbetter and the theft of Simon Devoreaux's film—before you wind up in real trouble."

Hennessy folded his arms over his chest and glared at the Hardys. "So who are you guys, anyway? The local police department? Next thing I know, you'll be threatening to drag me down to the station house if I don't confess." He assumed a wide-eyed look of innocence and said in a high-pitched voice, "Honest, officers, I don't remember a thing. Everything just went black, and then I woke up with a smoking gun in my hands."

The crowd laughed, but Frank didn't crack a smile. "We're serious, Mr. Hennessy. The people who are putting on this convention have asked us to find out who's responsible for stealing that film, and you've just given us our first solid clue."

Hennessy rolled his eyes. "Come on, you guys! You're taking me just a little bit too seriously. I was only kidding. Richard Feinbetter didn't take Simon Devoreaux's film. At least, I don't *think* he did."

"Then why did you say that he did?" Joe asked.

"It's a standing joke between Rich and me," Hennessy said. "He hates Simon Devoreaux and would love to get even with him someday. So when the film disappeared, well, the first person I thought about was Rich Feinbetter. But I don't really think he would do it. Rich is not a crook."

"What do you mean, 'get even'?" Frank asked. "Why would Feinbetter want to get even with Devoreaux?"

"Plagiarism," Hennessy said. There was a murmur from the crowd of fans surrounding Hennessy and the Hardys. "Ever since the first Galactic Saga film came out eight years ago, Rich has been claiming that Devoreaux was ripping off his books. And he's right. The Galactic Saga films bear a suspicious

44

resemblance to the Federation of Worlds series of novels that Rich published several decades ago, except that Rich's books were a lot better than Devoreaux's movies."

"Couldn't Feinbetter just take Devoreaux to court and sue him for plagiarism?" Joe asked.

"He could, and he did," Hennessy replied. "But the best lawyer that Rich Feinbetter could afford was nowhere near as good as the best lawyer—or team of lawyers—that Simon Devoreaux could afford. Devoreaux's lawyers made mincemeat out of Feinbetter's claims. They said the resemblances between the Galactic Saga movies and Feinbetter's books were coincidence, and they got away with it. All Feinbetter wanted was a small percentage of the profits from the films, but he never saw a cent."

"So now you think Feinbetter might want revenge?" Frank asked. He was aware of the crowd of fans who were watching him and his brother question Hennessy.

"Well . . ." Hennessy began, then he stared at the two teens through narrowed eyes. "Say, who are you two guys, anyway? You say the con committee hired you to find the culprit in the missing movie mystery?"

"Yes. We're investigating this crime," Joe said. "We help the police out sometimes with criminal cases in the Bayport area."

"Detectives, huh?" Hennessy said. "I thought you looked a little young to be cops. Well, don't take what I said about Rich Feinbetter too seriously. Dick may have reason to want revenge, but he's not the sort of guy who'd do something illegal to get it. Maybe he'd hire somebody to throw a pie in Devoreaux's face, but he wouldn't steal one of his films. I really *was* kidding when I said that."

"What about you?" Joe asked. "You just said some pretty nasty things about Devoreaux's films, too. You didn't happen to grab those movie reels from the limousine last night, did you?"

"Give me a break," Hennessy said. "I've been writing film reviews for the SF magazines for years. Unlike some of the fans at this convention, I happen to have good taste in movies, and Devoreaux's films leave a bad taste in my mouth. I've got nothing personal against the man, except for what he did to my friend Rich. And I also happen to think his movies are lousy."

"I see," Frank said, watching Hennessy carefully. Despite his comical attitude, the writer seemed sincere when he said he was innocent. "Well, if you happen to have any more thoughts about the theft, we'd appreciate it if you'd tell us about them," Frank added.

"Sure thing," Hennessy replied. As the Hardys turned and left the crowd, they heard Hennessy say, "They're making detectives younger all the time."

Frank and Joe looked at each other. It wasn't the first time they'd heard that comment.

"You know, I just thought of something," Frank said. "The guy in the space suit last night was tall.

Both Hennessy and Feinbetter are medium-size guys."

"That doesn't matter," Joe replied. "The guy we're looking for could have worn lifts in his shoes as part of his disguise."

"That's true," Frank admitted.

Just then the Hardys spotted Brian Amchick walking toward them.

"Hi, guys," Brian said with a smile. "How's it going?"

"We just had a close encounter with Arlen Hennessy," Frank said. "He's quite a comedian."

"That's Arlen," Brian said with a laugh.

"Listen," Joe said. "I've been thinking about the bootleg tape angle. If somebody wanted to sell bootleg copies of a science fiction movie on tape, where would he go? Would anybody be selling that kind of thing here at the convention?"

Brian thought about it for a moment. "Could be," he said finally. "I've seen that kind of thing floating around before. Sometimes you can recognize the bootleg tapes because they have hand-printed labels. The quality of the tapes usually isn't very good, either."

"Is there any place here at the convention where people sell videotapes and things like that?" Frank asked.

"Sure," Brian said. "The huckster room."

"The what?" Joe asked.

Brian laughed. "The huckster room. That's the place where all the dealers—the guys who sell books, films, posters, and stuff—set up tables. Every science fiction convention has one."

"Maybe we'd better check this out," Frank said. "Where is this huckster room?"

"Down in the basement," Brian said. "Come on. I'll show you."

Brian led them to a door at the far end of the lobby and down two flights of stairs. "The huckster room is right through here," he said.

He pushed open the door at the bottom of the stairs and followed the Hardys through. On the other side was a large room with unfinished concrete walls and high ceilings. On the floor were rows of metal tables, set up so that aisles ran between them. A man or a woman sat at each table, which had piles of merchandise on top. Fans strolled up and down the aisles, picking up the merchandise, examining it, and occasionally buying it.

"Pretty neat," Joe said, looking around. "Maybe I'll find some stuff here I want to buy."

The Hardys joined the browsing fans. Frank looked around and saw dealers selling everything from T-shirts with slogans such as "I'd Rather Be Time Traveling" to costumes modeled after those worn on a popular science fiction TV series. There were also piles and piles of old paperbacks with titles such as *The Changeling from Alpha Ten* and *The Million-Year War*.

"Where are the videotape dealers?" Frank asked Brian. "That's what we came down here to see."

"George Morwood's the guy you really ought to

talk to," Brian said. He scanned the room. "I think I see him over there."

Frank and Joe trailed behind Brian as he led them through the maze of tables. Finally they reached one that was stacked high with videotapes in brightly colored packages. Joe glanced over the table. Next to the videotapes he saw rows of movie posters and photos showing alien monsters and flying spaceships. Behind the table sat a man of about thirty-five, with a pale complexion and a distrustful look on his face.

Joe leaned toward Morwood and smiled. "Hi!" he said brightly. "We're looking for science fiction videotapes. You got any?"

With a scowling expression, Morwood looked Joe over, then gestured toward several rows of videotapes set up on the table. Joe began eagerly thumbing through them. Frank and Brian did the same.

Then Joe looked up at Morwood with a disappointed look on his face. "I think I've got all of these already," he said. "Don't you have anything, well, different? Something that's hard to find? Something that"—he leaned over the table and said in a whisper—"something that might not be available in the stores yet?"

Morwood seemed to consider Joe's words for a moment. Then he nodded faintly and reached under the table. He pulled out a tape and handed it to Joe.

"This one's brand-new," he said to Joe in a low voice. "You won't find it anywhere else. It's a real collector's item."

Joe studied the tape. The title of the film, *The*

*Nanotech Project*, was hand-lettered on a plain white label. Joe frowned at the label, then looked back at Morwood.

"Just how new is this?" he asked. "I mean, is it really, *really* new?"

"It's not even in the theaters yet," Morwood said. "You can't get any newer than that."

"That's pretty new, all right," Joe said. "You got any more films like this?"

Morwood looked at Joe suspiciously, a nervous expression on his face. "Why do you want to know?"

"I just want some new stuff for my tape collection," Joe said innocently. "That's all."

"You're not asking for anything . . . illegal, are you?" Morwood asked Joe. There was an edgy tone to his voice, and his eyes shifted around the room, as if he were checking whether anyone was watching.

Joe opened his eyes wide, as if he were shocked. "No!" he insisted. "I wouldn't even think of such a thing." He looked down at the tape in his hands. "This tape isn't illegal, is it?"

A frightened look crossed Morwood's face. He reached out and snatched the tape away from Joe. "I don't know what you're up to, kid," he said sharply, "but I run a legitimate business. And I don't like you insinuating things about the way I operate."

"Hey," Joe said, "I didn't mean to—"

"Sure you didn't," Morwood interrupted, putting the tape back under the table. "Now, get lost."

Frank gave Joe's shoulder a tug. "Come on, sport. I don't think you're making any friends here."

Joe moved away from the table. Brian and Frank followed after him.

"I don't like the looks of that guy," Joe muttered as soon as they were too far away to be heard. "He was pretty quick to pull that first tape out from under the counter when I asked for it. Then he got scared."

"You weren't exactly subtle," Frank said with a frown.

"I know," Joe admitted. "But that first tape sure looked like a pirate job to me. I guess I just pushed my luck too far. Maybe we should—"

"Hey," Frank interrupted. "Isn't that Richard Feinbetter?"

Joe looked in the direction Frank was pointing and saw the writer walking toward the exit. He was carrying a small stack of books that he had apparently purchased in the huckster room.

"Yeah, it is," Joe said. "Want to follow him and see where he goes?"

"Just what I was thinking," Frank said.

"Can I tag along?" Brian asked. "Sounds like fun."

"Be our guest," Frank said. "Just try to make yourself inconspicuous."

The Hardys and Brian waited until Feinbetter had closed the door to the stairs behind him. Then they walked up to the door and pushed it open. Feinbetter's footsteps echoed from above. Frank started climbing the stairs as quietly as he could, his brother and Brian a few steps behind him.

Feinbetter didn't exit the staircase at ground level. Instead, he kept climbing toward the higher floors.

51

Then Frank heard the footsteps come to an abrupt stop.

"Where'd he go?" Joe whispered. "I didn't hear a door open."

"I don't know," Frank said. "Let's go up to the next floor."

Frank and his companions crept up one more flight, only to find the door to the third floor still closed. Another flight of stairs led up to the fourth floor, but Frank could see no sign of Feinbetter.

"Some detectives we are," Frank said. "Can't even trail a suspect up the stairs."

Suddenly there was a sound from above. Frank looked up to see Feinbetter on the shadowy landing above them.

"Who are you?" the man snapped. "Why are you following me?"

He reached inside the front of the cardigan sweater he was wearing and pulled out a gun. He leveled it straight at the Hardys and Brian and said, "You'd better have a good answer to that question. Or else!"

# 6 Vanishing Act

Frank swallowed hard. For an older man, Feinbetter's gun hand was surprisingly steady, and the look on his face wasn't exactly friendly.

"Er, hello, Mr. Feinbetter," Frank stammered. "Hope you had a good time at the party last night."

Feinbetter squinted at Frank. "Now I recognize you," he said. "You're the two young men who were implying last night that I have something to do with the missing film."

"Sorry if we were a little out of line, sir," Joe said, his eyes on the gun. "Hope you didn't take it the wrong way."

"There seemed to be only one way to take it," Feinbetter retorted. "Who are you boys, anyway?

And why are you interested in Devoreaux's missing movie?"

Frank took a deep breath. "We're detectives, Mr. Feinbetter. We've been asked by the people who put on the convention to find the film."

"Maybe we should have business cards printed up," Joe suggested. "Then we wouldn't have to answer that question a zillion times a day."

"You really think I might have stolen the film?" Feinbetter asked.

"Well, you seem to have a motive," Frank replied.

"How would you know about that?" Feinbetter snapped.

"We, uh, heard a rumor," Joe said, "that you believe Simon Devoreaux ripped off some of your ideas in his Galactic Saga films."

Feinbetter rolled his eyes toward the ceiling. "I bet Arlen Hennessy told you about that. Arlen never did know when to shut up. And I suppose you're following me around the hotel to see if I meet with a fence to sell the stolen film. Correct?"

"That's about it, sir," Frank said.

"Well, I'm not," Feinbetter said. "I'm going up to my room to take a nap. I'm scheduled to be on two more panels this afternoon and evening, and at my age I need all the rest I can get. Do you have any objections to that?"

"No, sir," Joe said.

"I don't suppose you'd have any objections to putting down that gun?" Frank asked. "It's making us very nervous."

"Oh, this," Feinbetter said, looking down at the pistol in his hand. "Gave you a scare, did it?"

He aimed the gun directly at Frank, then pulled the trigger. Frank gasped and jumped backward, but all that came out of the gun was an orange flag that had the words "ZAP! You're star dust!" written on it.

"I bought this for my grandson," Feinbetter said with a grin. "Thought it was kinda cute."

Joe let out a sharp breath. "Another zap gun," he said. "Those things must be all over this con. It's so dark in this stairwell that I didn't recognize it."

"At least," Frank gasped, "this one didn't have a real gun hidden inside it."

"Now, if you boys will excuse me," Feinbetter said, "I'm going back to my room. And when I finish with my nap, I'm going to have a long talk with Arlen Hennessy."

"Yes, sir," Frank said as the writer disappeared through the doorway.

"Well, what do you think?" Frank said to Joe. "Do you think Feinbetter acts like the kind of guy who would have stolen Devoreaux's film?"

"How would I know?" Joe said with a shrug. "When's the last time we caught a crook who looked like a crook? Half the time the culprit turns out to be some perfectly innocent-looking person who helps little old ladies across the street. Sometimes it's even the little old lady."

"True," Frank said. "And Feinbetter never specifically denied taking the film. So far, he's got the best motive in the place."

55

"He definitely does," Joe agreed. "But I'm beginning to think that George Morwood might be in on this, too. Maybe they're in it together. Feinbetter stole the film, and Morwood plans to bootleg it."

"Maybe," Frank said. "What do you think about Morwood, Brian?" He turned and saw that Brian's face was completely white. He was staring at the Hardys, an awed expression on his face.

"Is this what you guys go through every day?" Brian asked. "Face people who point guns at you? If that had been a real gun, you could have gotten killed."

"Well, we don't run into guns every day," Frank said. "But it's not the first time, and sometimes the guns are real."

"Great," Brian said. "Maybe I shouldn't hang around you guys quite so much."

"I hope this doesn't scare you away," Joe said. "We really appreciate you taking us around the convention."

Brian glanced at his watch. "I know where I ought to be taking you right now. My uncle Pete is giving a presentation in about ten minutes. I promised him I'd be there."

"What's it about?" Joe asked. "I thought you said he was a professor at Boston Tech?"

"He is," Brian said, "so the presentation must have something to do with his specialty, computer science. Want to come watch?"

Joe frowned. "We really ought to be checking out

Feinbetter's room to see if he's got the stolen tapes hidden there."

"Except that Feinbetter's *in* his room right now," Frank said. "So let's go to the lecture. We might actually learn something."

"That's what I'm afraid of," Joe joked.

The three teenagers went back downstairs and through the lobby to one of the conference rooms. The room was already crowded with people, but the Hardys and Brian managed to find three seats together in the front row.

At the front of the room Joe saw Pete Amchick fiddling with a monitor attached to a video recorder. A variety of electronic instruments were strewn across the table next to the recorder. Finally the computer scientist stepped up to a microphone and cleared his throat.

"Good afternoon, ladies and gentlemen," he said. "I'm Pete Amchick. I know that a lot of you science fiction fans are interested in the subject of computer graphics. I've been doing a lot of work in that area, and I've brought along a presentation of some of my work. I'll be playing a short videotape for you. All of the images that you'll be seeing were generated by a computer."

Joe stifled a yawn. "This sounds about as fascinating as watching grass grow."

"We all know computers aren't your strong point," Frank said to his brother. "But try to stay awake, okay?"

Pete Amchick signaled to someone standing next to the door, and the lights began to dim. Then he pushed a button on the video recorder, and an image appeared on the monitor behind him.

Frank stared at the image, trying to decide exactly what it was. The truth was, he thought, that it didn't look like much of anything, just a white misty cloud swirling in front of a purple background. But then he noticed a small object in the center of the picture, growing rapidly larger, as though it were moving directly toward the viewer. As it grew, he saw that it was the planet Earth, spinning in space. It grew larger and larger until it filled the entire screen, and it kept right on growing.

Frank leaned forward in his seat and watched with growing fascination. It was as though he were in a spaceship hurtling down toward the surface of Earth. The ship zoomed directly in on the North American continent. Mountains and rivers began to appear, and then trees and roads and even buildings.

Frank turned to see his brother staring wide-eyed at the picture, too. "Wow!" Joe exclaimed. "Did he say he did this whole thing with a computer? It looks real."

Frank turned back to the monitor. His brother was right. It did look real. All the colors were brighter than he had ever seen before in a movie. The images were so clear they seemed to jump right off the screen at the audience.

The film was now rushing along the ground, past

trees and mountains. But Frank could see something else in the distance, something large and green. As it grew closer, he realized that it was a giant dinosaur—a fifty-story-tall *Tyrannosaurus rex* with green scales and dripping fangs. As the spaceship approached it, it seemed to sense their presence. It turned away from its meal and reached out toward the viewers with its slavering mouth and . . .

The spaceship suddenly took off into outer space, leaving the Tyrannosaurus far below. The blue sky changed to black, and stars began to twinkle. And then it appeared as though the viewers were racing *through* the stars, as if they were in a starship with a warp drive.

"This is better than a roller coaster," Joe whispered. "You didn't tell us your uncle was into wild stuff like this, Brian."

"He never mentioned it," Brian said. "I told you, Uncle Pete isn't very talkative."

"Hey, look," Frank said, his eyes never leaving the monitor. "It's a spaceship. Like the ones in the Galactic Saga movies."

A large silver spacecraft had appeared on the monitor. It was a saucerlike shape and had large engines shooting out streams of red particles to its rear. As the viewers flew toward it, the spaceship began to change shape. Like a lump of clay being molded in the hands of a sculptor, the spaceship became rounder. At one end a face appeared, while at the other end the craft seemed to grow feet. Fiery

59

eyes stared out from the monitor, and a mouth full of fangs appeared where the bridge of the spaceship had been.

The gaping mouth seemed to lunge at the viewers, and then they were inside the space monster, hurtling down into its metal gullet, sailing through its throat and into its stomach.

Then the picture went black, and large computer-style letters appeared. SORRY. YOUR JOURNEY HAS ENDED. YOU HAVE BEEN SWALLOWED BY A VORACIOUS GALACTIC TRANSFORMER DISGUISED AS A SPACESHIP. BETTER LUCK NEXT TIME.

Pete Amchick pushed a button, and the words vanished from the monitor. Somebody turned up the lights. There was a moment of silence, then the audience began to applaud loudly.

"That was terrific!" Joe shouted, jumping to his feet and clapping.

"I thought this was going to be as fascinating as watching grass grow," his brother said, looking up at him.

"Well, it wasn't exactly what I expected," Joe said.

Pete Amchick stepped up to the microphone, and the audience quieted down. He gave a brief speech, explaining that he was studying computer graphics techniques in order to create realistic images, and that this film was his most recent work.

"Can you produce any kind of image?" Frank asked. "Absolutely anything you want?"

"Pretty much," Pete answered. "We can show anything that we know how to write a program for.

All we have to do is feed the right data into the computer, and out pop images like the ones you just saw."

"Pretty impressive," Frank said.

Pete answered some more questions and demonstrated some of the electronic devices that were arrayed on the table. Finally the session came to an end, and the Hardys stood up to leave.

"Your uncle is a real whiz," Frank said to Brian.

"He sure is," Brian said. "Ever since I was a kid, I remember him building things. He has a robot that can travel around his apartment. It can even bring in the newspaper."

Joe led the way out of the room and into the hallway. He noticed that the afternoon crowd was getting larger and there were more and more people around in costume.

He turned to the others. "Anybody for lunch?" he asked.

"The motel coffee shop is right down this way," Brian said. "Follow me."

The coffee shop was large and about two-thirds filled with fans. Joe got a hamburger, and Frank and Brian bought subs. When they finished eating, they headed back toward the lobby.

"Speaking of lunch," Frank said, "weren't we supposed to be meeting Chet sometime soon?"

"Yeah," Joe said, looking around. "Maybe he decided to get into his costume for the masquerade contest later. I wonder if he—"

Joe stopped in midsentence, his gaze caught by

61

something in the hallway. Frank turned to see what his brother was looking at, but he saw only a fan in costume walking down the hallway toward them. The fan was dressed as a magician or sorcerer, with a pointed hat perched on his head and long, flowing black robes. His face was covered with a small mask and a long white beard.

Frank gasped when he saw there was a green medallion around his neck with a moon and star on it.

"That's him!" Joe shouted. "That's the guy who tricked me into using that broken elevator last night."

Joe shot forward, running toward the costumed fan. The magician stopped short, reached inside his robes, and pulled out a small object, which he threw directly at Joe's feet.

"What's going on?" Frank shouted.

With a loud poof a cloud of red and blue smoke filled the air, obscuring the Hardys' view of the costumed fan. Joe tried to run right through the smoke.

"Don't!" Frank cried. "That stuff might be poisonous." But his warning came too late. Joe was already in the middle of the smoke.

Suddenly the younger Hardy began to choke. He clutched a hand over his mouth and doubled over. With a strangling noise, Joe collapsed to the floor.

# 7 Maker of Worlds

Joe felt as if his lungs were going to burn right out of his chest. The brightly colored smoke had worked its way into his nose and mouth. He coughed desperately to push it back out, at the same time waving the smoke away from his face with his hand. Tears formed in his eyes, leaving him temporarily blinded.

He could hear the sound of the costumed fan running down the hallway toward the lobby, but there was nothing he could do to stop him.

Frank rushed to his brother's side and pulled him to his feet, out of the smoke.

"I got a—a real lungful of that stuff!" Joe exclaimed between coughs.

"Don't try to talk," his brother advised. "Cough it

63

out. That must have been some kind of smoke bomb."

"Catch that guy in the magician's outfit," Joe sputtered, "before he gets away."

Frank looked through the thinning clouds, but there was no sign of the person who had thrown the smoke bomb.

"I'm going to try to find him," Frank said. "Hang on. I'll be right back."

Waving the smoke away from his own face, Frank ran down the hallway in pursuit of Joe's attacker. When he reached the lobby, he saw that one of the elevator doors was just closing. He rushed over and banged on the button, trying to make the elevator door reopen, but it was no use. He watched the flashing lights above the elevator go all the way to the fourth floor, then stop. For a moment he considered running up the stairs in pursuit of the man with the medallion, but he knew that by the time he had climbed four flights of stairs, the magician would have disappeared. Feeling disgruntled, Frank headed back to the hallway, where Joe was waiting.

Brian was helping Joe stand up. "Are you okay, Joe?" he asked. "It looked like he got you pretty good with that stuff."

"I think I'll live," Joe said, straightening up with a groan. "Long enough to get revenge on that guy with the green medallion."

"I lost him again," Frank said, joining them. "Every time we meet that guy, he's in a different

64

costume and manages to give us the slip." He looked at his brother and Brian. "So, what do we do next?"

"We could check out Morwood," Joe said. "If we can find out what room he's staying in, we can look around for the missing film."

"I hate to suggest something frivolous," Brian said. "But Jack Gillis has been setting up an exhibit of props from the Galactic Saga movies out in the parking lot. It should be open by now."

"Oh, right," Frank said. "We saw him in his hovercar this morning."

"Well, I guess we can take a few minutes off from detective work and look at it," Joe said. "Anyway, I need some fresh air. Let's go."

The Hardys and Brian headed out to the parking lot, toward the green canvas tent. They saw a crowd of fans milling around the tent, going in and out of the open flap at one end.

Frank stepped through the flap and into the tent. The hovercar he had seen that morning was sitting on the ground, with a second hovercar next to it. Surrounding the hovercars were a number of items Frank recognized instantly from the Galactic Saga films, including scale models of various starships.

Suddenly a loud bellow caught Frank's attention. A live elephant dressed in battle gear stood to the rear of the tent. A masklike helmet draped over its head made it look like some kind of alien monster.

There was a stir of excitement from the fans. Frank looked over and saw Jack Gillis enter the tent and walk over to the elephant. "Hello, everybody," he said. "I see you've already met Bruno. He may look like an elephant, but actually he's a Surriband, one of the giant creatures that live in the desert of the planet Regnay. It's from the latest movie, *The Secret of Sigma Seven*. The one that you unfortunately didn't get to see last night."

"Is this the elephant that actually plays the part in the film?" someone asked.

Gillis laughed. "No, it's not. This is an elephant we borrowed from a local zoo. We're a little too far from Hollywood to bring the real elephant along with us. They'd probably charge us an extra fare on the airplane. But this *is* the actual costume that the elephant wears in the movie."

Frank began examining one of the scale model spaceships. It was remarkably detailed, with tiny windows that even had lights inside them and complex machinery poking out of the engines. It appeared to be made out of wood and plastic, though it had been painted to give it a metallic look.

"Are these models of the ships that you use in the Galactic Saga films?" Frank asked the special-effects director.

"No," Gillis replied. "Those are the actual ships. We use special camera techniques to make them look larger in the films."

"Incredible," Joe said. "They look so big in the movies."

"That's the magic of special effects," Gillis said, spreading his hands to indicate all the exhibits in the tent. "It's an art that I've been learning all my life, ever since I was making home movies as a kid. Something can look quite ordinary off camera, but if you photograph it right, it can look as if it's literally out of this world. A spaceship, for instance."

"Or an alien monster," Frank suggested.

"Or a whole planet," Joe said.

"Absolutely right." Gillis nodded his head. "I think of my job as the creation of worlds, and those worlds come alive on the movie screen."

"That must be a lot of fun," Frank said.

"Oh, it is," Gillis said, a warm grin spreading across his face. "I can't imagine doing anything else for a living."

"It must be quite an honor to work on the Galactic Saga movies," Brian said. "Some science fiction fans consider them the greatest SF movies ever made."

"Unless you talk to Arlen Hennessy," Joe said.

"I'm *very* honored to work on these films," Gillis said. "In many ways I regard them as my own creations as much as Simon Devoreaux's. Simon may be the one who puts the actors through their paces, but I get to build the universe around them."

"I'd like to know more about these hovercars," Joe said. "I don't suppose you can take one of them apart to show us how they work."

"No," Gillis said, chuckling. "But perhaps I can do you one better. Would you like to go for a ride with me in one of these cars?"

"You bet," Joe said.

"Then come on," Gillis said, walking to one of the

67

cars and hopping inside. "We'll take a turn around the parking lot."

Joe climbed in on the other side and sat down next to Gillis. The hovercar had bucket seats with padding that seemed to mold itself to Joe's body as he settled in. The dashboard looked to Joe like that of a sports car. Joe saw a key dangling out of the hovercar's ignition. Gillis reached up and turned the key. The hovercar jumped to life, rising into the air. Joe was surprised at how smooth it felt.

"Right now we're just hovering," Gillis said to Joe. "A high-speed column of air blows out of the bottom of this vehicle, holding us aloft. To make the car move, we need to use this."

Gillis put his hand on a rod that stuck up from the floor of the car and yanked it gently toward the rear. Joe felt a gentle vibration shoot through the car as it started moving backward toward the end of the tent.

"This looks like a gearshift," Gillis said. "But actually it's more like a joystick. I push it in the direction I want the car to go and . . . it goes."

He pulled it back more sharply, and the hovercar moved in the direction he pushed it, through the open flap of the tent. Joe felt himself bucked forward in his seat as Gillis guided the car into the parking lot, barely missing a group of fans who were coming in to see the exhibition.

Gillis laughed as he nimbly guided the car around them. "Now we'll go forward," he said, pushing the joystick toward the front of the vehicle. The car reversed direction, and Joe was thrown backward

68

into the soft padding of the seat. Gillis raced ahead into an empty area of the parking lot. Joe threw his head back and laughed out loud. Gillis rocketed around a group of parked cars, then swung the hovercar back in the direction of the tent. Joe was swung from side to side in his seat as Gillis changed direction, and it felt as though he were moving at a very high speed. But when Joe looked around, he realized that was an illusion. They probably weren't going any faster than thirty miles per hour.

"I love it!" he cried, the wind blowing through his hair. "This is it. I'm buying one of these as soon as it hits the market."

"You'll have to wait only about a hundred years," Gillis said, guiding the car back to the flap of the tent. "We don't have any plans to market these things, unfortunately. It's not a very practical vehicle, I'm afraid."

Gillis turned off the engine and let the car settle back to the ground just outside the tent. A crowd of fans immediately gathered around it as Joe climbed out.

"That was a blast and a half," Joe declared, rejoining Frank. "What happened to Brian?" he asked.

"He had to meet some friends inside the motel," Frank explained. "He'll catch up with us later."

Several other fans were clustered around Gillis, asking to be given a ride around the parking lot. But the special-effects director begged off.

"I'm sorry, but you'll have to wait until later," he

69

said. "I'm knocking off now to get a late lunch. I'll be back in about an hour, with free rides for all."

"But you just got here," Joe said.

"I've had a busy day," Gillis said. "The con committee has been asking me to put in appearances all over the convention."

Gillis chased the last fans out of the tent, then closed the flap and latched it shut. As the crowd of fans thinned out, Gillis started heading back toward the motel. Frank and Joe glanced at each other, then back at the director.

"Uh, could we speak with you for a moment, Mr. Gillis?" Frank asked. "We'll try not to keep you from your lunch for long."

Gillis turned and looked at the brothers. "Is it important? I really do want to get something to eat."

"It's about the theft of that film last night," Frank said. "We're investigating it for the people who put on the convention, and we'd just like to ask you a couple of questions."

Gillis's face fell. "Oh, yes. Simon told me that the con committee had asked a couple of detectives to look for the missing film. It's a terrible incident, isn't it? I know a lot of people were looking forward to seeing the premiere last night. I was going to give a speech afterward, with Simon, but we never had a chance. Fortunately, there's still a master negative back in Hollywood. But there's no time to make a new copy to show here at the convention."

"Do you have any idea who might have taken it?"

Joe asked. "Do you think somebody's making bootleg copies of the movie? Or does somebody have a grudge against Simon Devoreaux? Remember that someone tried to kill him last night."

"There's always the possibility of bootlegging," Gillis said. "I remember after the last movie came out, there were bootleg videotapes available from dealers within a week of the release. We've never had a film stolen *before* it was released, though. I should imagine a bootleg copy of an unreleased Galactic Saga film would be worth quite a bit of money."

"That's what we thought, too," Frank said. "Do you know of any bootleggers operating in this area?"

"Afraid not," Gillis said. "I try not to involve myself in that side of the business. And as for anybody having a grudge against Simon, well, that's always a possibility. Simon isn't the most diplomatic man around, and he's made a few enemies over the years, but I can't imagine any of them would strike out at him in this manner. Now, if that answers your questions, I really do have to eat lunch."

"Sure," Joe said. "Thanks, Mr. Gillis. You've been a big help."

Gillis nodded at the brothers and started walking back toward the motel. Suddenly, as he walked away, the Hardys heard a hovercar fan revving up.

Joe turned to see the hovercar he had been riding moments earlier lift from the ground and start to move. The fans that lifted it into the air made a loud

71

hissing noise as the car floated above the ground. Then, as if it had a mind of its own, it suddenly shot forward at its fastest speed.

As Joe watched, Gillis began to turn toward the sound of the hovercar. He had a stunned expression on his face, as if he couldn't believe what he was seeing.

Joe couldn't believe his eyes, either. The hovercar was heading directly toward Jack Gillis!

# 8 The Missing Master

"Mr. Gillis!" Joe shouted as the hovercar rocketed toward the special-effects director. "Look out!"

Gillis started to turn, but it was obvious that he would never be able to get out of the hovercar's path in time. Frank leaped forward and tackled Gillis around the waist, knocking him to the pavement of the parking lot. The hovercar shot by a few inches overhead and plowed into the wall of the motel. It bounced away, deflected by the rubber bumpers that surrounded the lower rim of the car, then settled back to the ground.

"What happened?" Gillis gasped.

"You were almost the victim of a runaway hovercar," Frank said, climbing back to his feet. He reached down and helped Gillis stand up.

"What?" Gillis said in disbelief. He turned and saw the hovercar lying next to the building. "Oh, no!" he exclaimed. "It must have gone out of control!"

He rushed over to the hovercar and examined it. "It doesn't seem to have been damaged. I don't know how the car could have gone out of control like that."

"There wasn't anybody around it," Joe said. "It just started moving—straight at you."

"Is there any way to remote-control the car?" Frank asked. "Could someone have started it from a distance?"

"No," Gillis said firmly, opening a small hoodlike compartment at the front of the hovercar. "It can be started and controlled only from inside. It must have been some kind of glitch in the machinery. Or"— his voice changed tone—"somebody's been tampering with the mechanism."

Gillis studied the engine carefully. "I don't see anything unusual," he finally said, closing the hood. "I'll give it a complete checkup later." He got into the hovercar, started it up, and drove it back to the tent. Then he climbed out and walked back to Frank and Joe.

"Well, I'm a little shaken up by that," Gillis told the Hardys, "but I still have to eat lunch. Maybe some food will calm my nerves."

"You'd better be careful, Mr. Gillis," Joe said. "It looks like somebody may be trying to hurt you as well as Mr. Devoreaux."

74

"I'll take care," Gillis said. He left them and walked back toward the motel.

"He's a pretty cool character," Joe said as the brothers headed across the parking lot toward the motel, keeping a distance behind Gillis. "I might be too shaken up to eat lunch if somebody just tried to kill me."

"Somebody tried to kill you last night when you left the party, and I didn't notice it had any effect on your appetite," Frank observed.

"True," Joe said thoughtfully. "But I'm used to it. I've been in the detective business for a while."

"Well, maybe Gillis is used to it," Frank said. "After all, he deals with complicated mechanical devices like the hovercar every day. Maybe this sort of thing happens a lot in the movie business. Do you believe that thing started all by itself?" he asked his brother.

"No," Joe said. "Too much of a coincidence. Last night somebody tried to kill Simon Devoreaux, and this afternoon somebody tried to kill Jack Gillis."

"Sounds like somebody wants not only to snatch Devoreaux's latest film," Frank said, walking on, "but also to get rid of the entire team as well. You suppose they'll go after the actors next?"

"Fortunately, the actors aren't at this convention," Joe said. "Which probably greatly increases their life expectancies."

Frank thought for a moment. "Do you suppose," he said, "that it would increase the value of a bootleg

75

film if the people who were in charge of the movie—such as the director, the writer, the special-effects supervisor—were all out of the way, so they couldn't remake the film?"

Joe laughed. "That's the craziest idea I've ever heard! Crazy . . . and kind of scary, too."

"All right," Frank said. "How many suspects do we have?"

"Everybody who was in this motel last night," Joe said. "And probably a few who weren't."

"Let's narrow it down a bit," Frank said. "Who do we know that has a motive?"

"George Morwood, for one," Joe said. "He's my favorite. He deals in videotapes of popular science fiction films and may have some shady dealings going. He'd probably love to get his hands on a copy of Devoreaux's film so he can sell bootleg copies of it." Joe opened the door and stepped into the motel.

"But we still don't know why he would try to kill Devoreaux and Gillis," Frank said as he settled into one of the thickly padded sofas in the middle of the lobby.

"You know, I was thinking . . ." Joe said, sitting in a chair opposite his brother. "The stolen copy isn't really worth that much if the master is still in Hollywood. You heard what Gillis said about there being a master negative under lock and key."

"Right," Frank said.

"Let's assume that Morwood also stole the master film," Joe said, propping his feet on a coffee table. "Maybe he wants to guarantee that nobody can remake the film from scratch. If Devoreaux and Gillis, the two major creative talents behind the film, are out of the way and the master negative is gone, Morwood would have the only copy of *The Secret of Sigma Seven* that will ever exist. It can't be refilmed by its creators, and nobody can make a new copy because the master negative is gone. The only existing copy would be worth a fortune to collectors."

"Those are pretty big assumptions," Frank said. "How would Morwood get to the master negative in Hollywood? He's been here in the motel all weekend."

"Good question," Joe admitted. He paused to think over the problem.

"It sounds unlikely to me," Frank said. "And I'm not so sure about the idea that the thief wants to kill Devoreaux and Gillis to keep them from remaking the film. It costs a lot of money to make a movie, particularly a movie with a lot of special effects. I can't see the studio agreeing to finance a remake, especially if there are bootleg copies around."

"I guess you're right," Joe said. "But it's something to keep in mind."

"Now, what about Richard Feinbetter?" Frank asked. "Think he might have done it?"

"Possibly," Joe said. "He's got a motive, too. He thinks Devoreaux's been ripping him off all these years."

Frank stared thoughtfully out the window at the parking lot. "Feinbetter hates Devoreaux," Frank mused, "but he doesn't necessarily hate Gillis."

"We don't know that he doesn't," Joe said. "Remember what Gillis said about how the Galactic Saga movies are as much his creation as Devoreaux's?"

Frank nodded. "We certainly can't rule Feinbetter out. So that gives us two suspects. And I wouldn't be surprised if we find some more before the day is out."

"Why would we want more suspects?" Joe asked. "We're supposed to be narrowing down the list."

"I know," Frank said. "But the list always has a way of growing before it gets shorter." He glanced over his brother's shoulder. "Speaking of suspects, look who's on his way out of the motel."

Joe turned to see George Morwood, the videotape dealer that they had met in the huckster room earlier, approach the door with a large box in his hands. Inside was a jumbled pile of videotape cartridges.

The Hardys stood up and walked over to him. When Morwood saw Frank and Joe coming toward him, he quickly pushed the door open and hurried away.

"Excuse me, Mr. Morwood?" Frank said as he and Joe followed the dealer outside. "Can we talk to you again for a minute?"

"No," Morwood snapped, walking at a rapid pace toward the parking lot. "I don't want anything to do with you guys. Not after this morning."

"Aw, give us a break, Mr. Morwood," Joe said. "It wasn't anything personal. We're just investigating the theft of that film, that's all."

"Well, you've got no reason to investigate me," Morwood said in a huffy tone of voice. "I didn't have anything to do with it, and that's all you need to know. Now, if you'll excuse me . . ."

Morwood pulled open the rear door of a large van and placed the box of tapes inside. Then he closed the door and walked around to the front. He climbed into the driver's seat, started up the engine, and drove away, leaving the Hardys alone in the middle of the parking lot.

"We'd better keep our eye on him," Frank said. "If he's got the film, he must have it hidden someplace. Maybe he'll lead us to it eventually."

"Maybe he's taking it away in that van right now," Joe said.

Frank shook his head. "I doubt it," he said. "Not in broad daylight. He'd probably be afraid someone would see him."

"This would be a good time to check out Morwood's room, while he's gone," Joe said.

"We don't know where he's staying," Frank pointed out. "He might not even be rooming in the motel."

"It wouldn't be hard to find out," Joe said. "We'll just ask at the desk and tell them that we're friends of his. It's an old trick, but it usually works."

"Okay," Frank said, turning back toward the motel. "And maybe it's about time we talked to Simon Devoreaux, too."

"We should have talked to him before now," Joe said as he followed his brother. "But the guy's impossible to get close to. He's always got those bodyguards around him. And he doesn't look particularly friendly."

"We'll just have to figure out a way to get to him," Frank said.

The Hardys entered the motel. The registration desk was located next to the elevators, and it took the brothers only a minute to learn that George Morwood was in room 137. They thanked the woman at the desk and headed down the hallway past the elevators.

When they reached Morwood's room, Joe paused in front of the door. He looked both ways to see if anyone was watching, then pulled a Swiss army knife out of his pocket.

"This looks like a pretty easy lock," he said to his brother. "Tell me if you see anybody coming." He picked out the little screwdriver from the knife and poked it into the lock mechanism. A moment later there was a click. Joe turned the knob and opened the door.

Joe stepped inside the room, followed by Frank. He closed the door carefully, then looked around. Morwood wasn't much of a housekeeper, Joe noted. Clothes were scattered on the floor, on the dressers, and on top of the messy bed. Boxes full of videocassettes were stacked on the floor.

"Maid service must not have been here yet," Frank said.

"They ought to get time and a half for doing this room," Joe said.

The brothers searched briskly through the clothing and piles of videotapes but found nothing suspicious. Frank opened the door to the closet, but there was nothing inside except a few unused hangers.

"A lot of good this did us," Frank said. "If Morwood's got the film, he knows better than to keep it in here."

"And I don't see any sign of a porcupine costume," Joe said. "Or an astronaut's suit. Or the famous green medallion. Come on, let's get out of here."

Joe led his brother back into the hallway, closing the door behind him. As they headed down to the lobby, they saw Linda Klein, the convention official who had asked them to investigate the theft, coming in the opposite direction. She was walking quickly, with a stricken look on her face.

"Hey, Linda," Frank said. "Any news about Devoreaux's film?"

She stopped walking and looked up at Frank. "Yes, we've had news," she said glumly. "And it's worse than ever."

"What happened?" Joe asked.

"Word just came in from Hollywood," she replied. "The master negative of *The Secret of Sigma Seven* has been stolen."

# 9 Thunder and Lightning

Joe looked at his brother. "It looks as if one of my theories was right," he said grimly.

"If somebody's trying to corner the market on copies of *The Secret of Sigma Seven*, they're sure doing a good job," Frank commented.

"And just when I thought I had Simon Devoreaux talked out of suing us," Linda said with a groan. "He had even agreed to appear on a panel tonight at seven o'clock with Richard Feinbetter and several other writers. Devoreaux probably won't speak to me again when he hears what happened to the master negative."

"You mean he hasn't heard yet?" Joe asked.

"No," Linda replied, pushing up her glasses. "He's not taking any calls in his suite right now, so the studio sent the message to the convention committee. I answered all the calls myself. I'm just going up to deliver the message to Devoreaux now."

Suddenly her eyes lit up. "Wait a minute!" she cried. "I don't have to deliver this message to Devoreaux right now."

"You don't?" Joe asked.

"No," she said, a gleeful look on her face. "I'll just hold on to the news until tomorrow—until *after* he's been on the panel tonight."

"Won't he be madder than ever when he finds out?" Frank asked.

"Yeah," Joe added. "Then he might be twice as ready to sue you."

"Wrong," she said, fixing her gaze on Frank and Joe. "Because you two are going to find the person who stole the film before then."

Frank stared at Linda in astonishment. "We are? I mean, of course we're going to find the guy. But what if we don't find him before you have to give the message to Devoreaux?"

Linda Klein shook her head and smiled. "I've heard a lot about how good you guys are. You've caught lots of crooks, ones that even the police couldn't find. So you can catch this guy by tomorrow, right?"

"Well," Joe said, "we'll try our best."

"I'm sure that'll be good enough," Linda said. "How's it coming? Have you figured out who the thief is yet?"

"We've found some clues but—" Frank began.

"Great!" Linda exclaimed. "Keep up the good work. I've got complete faith in you two. I'll just hold on to this message until tomorrow. I'm sure Mr. Devoreaux doesn't want to be worried right now, anyway."

"I'm sure," Joe said in a doubtful tone.

"Do you think there's any chance we can talk to Simon Devoreaux himself?" Frank asked Linda. "He might be able to give us some important clues."

A worried look crossed Linda's face. "Talk to Devoreaux? You don't really want to talk to him, do you?"

"Well, yes, we do," Frank replied. "Unless you really don't want us to find the missing film."

"I don't want *anybody* talking to Simon Devoreaux right now!" Linda said emphatically. "I've managed to get him calmed down for a while, and I don't want anybody upsetting him. He's one of those guys with a hair-trigger temper. You never know what might set him off."

"It would really help us if we could talk—" Joe began.

"No," Linda said firmly. "Absolutely not. You guys are sharp enough to solve this crime without talking to Simon Devoreaux. Now, listen, I've got some convention business to take care of. I'll see you guys later, right?"

"Right," Joe said as Linda Klein disappeared down the hallway.

"For a woman whose neck is on the line, she could be a little more helpful," Frank commented.

"I know," Joe said. "She seems to think we can perform miracles."

"Well, she's right about that," Frank said with a grin. "The question is, can we perform them fast enough?"

"By the way," Joe said, "is something wrong with my ears, or did I hear her say that Devoreaux and Richard Feinbetter are appearing on a panel together tonight?"

"That's what she said, all right," Frank said.

"So what do you think's going to happen when those two guys get together?" Joe asked.

"I think sparks are going to fly," Frank said. "Somebody ought to tell Linda that those two are old enemies and will probably try to kill each other before the night's over."

"Think we should be the ones to tell her?" Joe asked his brothers.

A wicked gleam appeared in Frank's eye. "Nah! But I think we should show up for the panel. It ought to be fun. Who knows? Either Feinbetter or Devoreaux might say or do something that will help us with the case."

"Good idea," Joe said.

Just then the Hardys glimpsed a startling apparition coming down the hallway toward them. It was eight feet tall and covered with bright red feathers. Two things resembling both arms and wings flapped up and down against its sides. At its throat was a hole, like the opening of a pouch, and out of that hole suddenly popped a head.

"Hi, guys," Chet announced. "How do you like my costume?"

Joe stared at Chet, dumbfounded. "Uh, I'm having a little trouble putting my thoughts into words."

"I thought you were going as the Zepton poodle, Chet," Frank said. "What made you change your mind?"

"That costume was too hot," Chet said. "So I traded it for this one. How do you like it?"

"What's it supposed to be?" Joe asked. "A radio-active rooster?"

"I don't know," Chet said with a shrug of his feathered shoulders. "But it sure looks neat, doesn't it?"

"If you say so, Chet," Frank said. He was having trouble keeping a straight face.

Suddenly Chet plunged forward, and Frank and Joe managed to catch him just before he struck the floor.

"Whoa!" Chet cried. "I'm still having a little trouble with these stilts. Can't keep my balance."

"Are you really sure wearing this costume is a good idea?" Joe asked.

"Definitely," Chet said, nodding. "The masquerade contest is at eight o'clock tonight. I'm sure to win in this outfit. You guys are coming, aren't you?"

Joe thought about it for a minute. "That's right after the panel this evening. I guess we can drop by."

"Everybody's going to love this costume," Chet said, "though it's pretty hot inside this one, too. In fact, all this heat is making me hungry. You guys want to go for an early dinner?"

"Somehow I suspected you wouldn't forget dinner," Frank said. "You're not going in that costume, though, are you?"

"I guess I can take off the stilts," Chet said. "But it took me so long to get into this thing, I don't want to take it off so soon before the contest."

Chet slipped the stilts out from inside the costume and slung them over his shoulder. He then took one step forward and plunged to the floor.

"Having a little trouble walking, Chet?" Joe asked, offering his friend a hand.

"I just tripped over my feathers," Chet said.

"Maybe Joe could grab your feet and I could grab your shoulders," Frank suggested, "and we'll haul you to dinner."

Just before seven o'clock the Hardys and Chet met Brian at the door of the conference room where the panel was taking place.

"From what you guys tell me about Feinbetter and Devoreaux," Brian said, "this should be quite a panel."

"It'll be interesting seeing those two together, that's for sure," Joe agreed.

The four teenagers entered the room. Frank looked around and saw that it was about two-thirds full. A long table with five chairs behind it had been set up at the front of the room. In front of each chair was a microphone and a place card with a name on it. Frank, Joe, and Brian sat in the sixth row, along with Chet, who was still dressed in his giant bird costume.

At seven o'clock sharp Feinbetter and Hennessy entered the room and took seats behind the table. Frank watched as they were joined a moment later by a man and a woman. Frank didn't recognize them, but Brian seemed to be familiar with them.

The four panelists sat behind the table for a few moments as the clock ticked past seven. In one corner of the audience Frank saw Linda Klein look nervously at her watch, then glance at the door.

"I wonder if Devoreaux is going to show up," Joe said. "Maybe he found out about that stolen master negative and blew his stack."

"Linda Klein looks really nervous," Frank said. "I would be, too, if I were in her shoes."

"Jack Gillis is here," said Joe, pointing toward the front row. "That's a good sign. He probably wouldn't bother to attend this if Devoreaux wasn't going to show."

At that moment the door of the room burst open and Devoreaux walked in. Frank recognized the director's bodyguards and the rest of his entourage following directly behind him. As Devoreaux took a seat behind the table next to Arlen Hennessy, the bodyguards sat in the front row of seats directly opposite him. Frank saw Feinbetter lean forward and glare at the director, but Devoreaux completely ignored the writer.

"Hey, Uncle Pete's here," Brian said, nodding toward the door. "I wondered if he was going to show up."

Frank followed Brian's gaze. Pete Amchick was standing just inside the door. "Think he's still looking for a chance to talk with Simon Devoreaux?" Frank asked Joe.

"Good question," Joe said. "I wonder what that's about, anyway? Devoreaux's bodyguards would probably turn him into hamburger meat if he tried to get anywhere near the great man."

Arlen Hennessy, seated in the center of the table, began to speak. "I've been asked by Linda Klein to be the moderator of this panel," he said. "The subject tonight is galactic empires. The writers—and director—at this table have been chosen for their expertise on that subject. I don't write books about galactic empires, so I'll let the others do the talking. For a change."

There was an appreciative chuckle from the audience. Hennessy smiled in return and said, "We'll start with the man who has turned galactic empires into a multimillion-dollar industry. I'm sure that the director of the Galactic Saga movies needs no introduction to the fans in this room. Mr. Devoreaux, would you like to say a few words about what inspired you to create a series of movies about a perpetually warring galactic empire?"

"Uh-oh," Joe whispered. "You don't suppose Hennessy is deliberately bringing up a subject that will get Feinbetter and Devoreaux at each other's throats do you?"

"I bet that's exactly what he's doing," Frank said. "We came here to watch some fireworks, and we're about to get them."

Devoreaux cleared his throat and leaned forward, his deeply tanned face contrasting sharply with the pale white walls of the room. "This is a story I've told many times," he said into his microphone. To Frank, the director's tone of voice sounded more than a little arrogant. "But I suppose there's no harm in telling it again. I was inspired to create the Galactic Saga after a particularly vivid dream I had one night, in which godlike powers were warring for control of the very stars themselves."

"You didn't happen to have that dream after reading one of my books, did you?" Richard Feinbetter muttered.

"Excuse me, Mr. Feinbetter?" Devoreaux said, turning slowly toward the writer, who was seated on the other side of Hennessy. "Did you wish to make a comment?"

"I don't think any comments are necessary," Feinbetter replied, looking Devoreaux in the eye. "You're such an obvious fraud, after all."

Devoreaux's gaze remained steady. "I see you're still making your old accusations, Mr. Feinbetter," he said. "I don't suppose you'd like to come right out and state your grievances?"

"I've stated them plenty of times before,"

Feinbetter snapped angrily. "I think you've pla-
giarized my novels, and you keep plagiarizing
them every time you make a new Galactic Saga
movie."

"You realize that statement verges on libel, don't
you?" Devoreaux accused.

"I don't care. It's the truth, and the truth can
never be libelous," Feinbetter said. "You're a thief
and a liar, and there's no question in my mind about
it."

Devoreaux's face turned purple with rage. "Listen, Feinbetter," he said, rising from his chair. "I've
put up with your ridiculous accusations for the
better part of a decade now, and I've had just about
enough——"

As Frank watched in surprise, Simon Devoreaux
suddenly lunged toward Richard Feinbetter. Arlen
Hennessy stood up to block the sudden attack, but
Devoreaux reached around him and grabbed
Feinbetter's jacket.

At that moment the room filled with the sound of
rolling thunder, which Frank realized was booming
out of loudspeakers mounted on the ceiling overhead. Devoreaux froze in place as a deep voice rose
above the thunder and began rumbling in sinister
tones, "Simon Devoreaux, prepare to meet your
maker!"

A crackling bolt of lightning appeared out of
nowhere. It shot down from the ceiling, making a
noise so loud that Frank instinctively covered his

ears. The bolt zipped right past Simon Devoreaux, singeing the hairs on his neck, and struck the chair where he had been sitting just a second before.

As Frank watched, startled, Devoreaux's chair burst into flames!

# 10 The Pressure Mounts

Frank and Joe leaped to their feet. The conference room was in an uproar. Frank saw the panelists throw their chairs aside and race for the aisle that ran down the center of the room, while the audience members vaulted out of their seats and looked around to see if any lightning bolts were likely to come flying in their direction. Frank heard a fire alarm go off as the smoke from Devoreaux's burning chair rose toward the ceiling. Suddenly a burst of water came spraying out of the sprinkler system on the ceiling, most of it raining down on the front of the room.

A number of people in the audience began to file noisily out of the room. Frank saw that Simon Devoreaux was still standing behind the table. The director was staring down at the burning chair in which he had been sitting in only seconds before. Frank could see flames shooting upward from the scorched chair, but they were being quickly doused by the sprinklers. Water ran down Devoreaux's ashen face and onto his suit jacket.

Devoreaux's stunned bodyguards finally leaped into action. They rushed over to their employer and tried to shield him with their bodies, but there was nothing left to protect him from except the streams of water from the sprinkler. No more lightning came bolting out of the blue.

"Where did that bolt of lightning come from?" Joe asked, looking toward the table.

Frank pointed at the ceiling. "Look up there."

Joe looked upward. In the center of the ceiling, partially hidden by a large chandelier, a small black box hung down. Thin black wires trailed off it. The other ends of the wires were connected to the electrical system at the base of the chandelier. Streams of smoke trailed away from the box and dissipated into the air.

"What is it?" Joe asked.

"Must be some sort of electrical device," Frank said. "And look over there."

He pointed at the floor near the panelists' table. Barely visible under the scorched remains of Simon Devoreaux's chair was a second black box.

"That must have been there all along," Frank said, "but we didn't notice it. The lightning leaped from one box to the other, using the building's electrical system as a power source. Those boxes have probably been building up an electrical charge for hours. Somebody pressed a button or something and released it."

"Who do you suppose rigged up a device like that?" Joe asked. "He'd have to be a real electronics whiz."

Frank's eye fell on a small table toward the back of the room. Several electronic gadgets, left over from Pete Amchick's earlier demonstration, were still sitting there. Amchick himself was sitting in the corner of the room, a calm expression on his face.

"I hate to say it, but . . ." Frank began.

Joe followed Frank's gaze. "You're not going to suggest that Pete Amchick was responsible for this, are you? Why would he want to kill Simon Devoreaux? Or Jack Gillis? For that matter, why would he want to steal the film?"

"Why did he want to talk to Devoreaux?" Frank asked. "Brian's uncle has been acting awfully mysterious, and he's an electronics wizard. Remember that Brian said he keeps a robot around his apartment? Maybe we should have been watching him a little more closely."

Frank glanced at Brian, but the young man didn't seem to notice that Joe and Frank were talking about his uncle. Brian and Chet were busy discussing the strange events of the last few moments.

Just then two security guards rushed into the room. One was carrying a fire extinguisher, which he

95

sprayed at the pile of debris next to Simon Devoreaux, even though it was no longer on fire. The other guard turned to the people who remained and told them that the fire department would be arriving in a few minutes and that they should exit the room in an orderly fashion.

"We'd better get out of here," Joe said.

"Maybe we can talk to Devoreaux out in the hall," Frank suggested.

"I doubt it," Joe said, nodding toward the front of the room, where the bodyguards were ushering the director down the center aisle. "Those two guys aren't letting anybody near him. But maybe we can talk to Pete Amchick, if he's willing to talk to us. He seemed like a pretty closemouthed fellow."

Frank grabbed Chet's shoulder and found himself with a handful of feathers. "Come on, you guys," he said, shaking off the feathers. "Let's go."

"Uh, Brian," Joe said as they headed for the door, "do you think your uncle Pete would mind talking to us?"

"I don't see why not," Brian said. "What about?"

Joe briefly considered telling Brian the truth, then decided there was no reason to upset him as long as they had no concrete evidence against his uncle. "Oh, just about those computer graphics he showed us this afternoon," he said. "We thought they were really great."

"And I want to ask his opinion about that lightning device that almost zapped Simon Devoreaux back there," Frank said. "Maybe he knows a few things about how that might work."

"I bet he does," Brian said. "Uncle Pete's a real electrical genius."

Joe saw Brian's uncle following Simon Devoreaux and his bodyguards out the door, but once again Amchick was unable to get anywhere near the director. Brian hurried after his uncle and tapped him on the shoulder.

"Uncle Pete?" he asked. "Got a minute? My friends here want to talk to you."

"No time," Pete muttered. "I've got to catch up with Simon Devoreaux. I've been trying to talk to him all day." As Devoreaux and his entourage disappeared down the hallway, Pete Amchick hurried after him.

"That guy never gives up," Frank said. "I wish I could figure out what he wants to talk to Devoreaux about."

"Me, too," Brian said. "I have to admit, he's acting even weirder than usual."

By the time they reached the lobby, somebody had posted notices announcing that the costume party would be held at eight o'clock in a different conference room, because of the fire.

"All right!" Chet declared. "Here's my chance to shine. Anybody know where I left my stilts?"

Two hours later the Hardys, Chet, and Brian left the costume party. "That was really fun," Joe said.

"Too bad you didn't win the Cosmic Costume Contest, Chet."

"You probably blew your chances when your stilts broke as you were crossing the room and you collided with the guy dressed as a flying saucer," Frank said.

"That shouldn't have made any difference," Chet insisted. "I still think my costume was better than the three-headed Uranian gerbil monster. I don't think that should have won second prize, a year's subscription to *Other Worlds* magazine."

"Well, you must admit that the nine guys dressed as a giant octopus were pretty awesome," Joe said. "Which is why they won the trip to Cape Canaveral."

"Listen," Brian said as the Hardys and Chet prepared to leave the con for the evening. "I reserved a room in the motel for the weekend so that I could spend more time at the convention. Do you guys want to crash on the floor tonight? You can get an early start in the morning."

"No, thanks," Joe said. "We've been going nonstop all day, and I'm looking forward to sleeping in my own bed."

"Uncle Pete will be there," Brian said. "He crashed there last night, too. He's so absentminded he never bothered to reserve a motel room here, and now they're all booked up."

Frank gave Joe a glance. "Maybe you should think twice, Joe. It might be fun to spend the night on Brian's floor."

"Uh, yeah," Joe said. "Hope your uncle Pete won't mind a little conversation."

"I'm sure he won't," Brian said.

When they reached Brian's room, Pete Amchick was already there, poring over some papers at a small writing desk. He looked up briefly at Brian and his friends as they entered the room.

"Excuse me, Professor Amchick," Frank said, "can we talk with you for a minute?"

"I've got some things I need to look over," Pete said. "Perhaps some other—"

"It'll just take a minute," Joe interrupted. He told Brian's uncle about the black boxes he and Frank had seen in the conference room. "We were wondering if you could tell us anything about how the lightning bolt was generated."

A spark of interest appeared in Amchick's eyes. "Oh, yes. Fascinating device. Of course, I've never seen its inner workings, but I can make a few guesses." He began talking about electric potential and a number of other subjects. Frank felt more confused when Pete Amchick finished speaking than when he had begun.

"That's all very interesting," Joe said when Amchick finally finished his lecture. "Do you think you could build something like that?"

"Probably," Amchick said. "I suppose I could find all the necessary parts at the university. Why do you ask?"

"Oh, we were just curious," Frank said. "I bet

Simon Devoreaux would like to know a little more about that gadget that almost zapped him."

"Have you gotten a chance to speak to Devoreaux yet, Mr. Amchick?" Joe asked.

"No," Pete Amchick said calmly. "But that's because of the unfortunate events of this weekend. I'm sure that when all of this calms down, he'll be willing to speak to me."

"What exactly is it you want to talk to him about?" Joe asked.

"The matter is private," Amchick said. With that, he turned back to his books and ignored the Hardys.

Joe and Frank looked at each other with expressions of frustration, then began to get ready for bed.

The next morning Joe awoke with a groan. He had slept on the floor at the foot of Brian's twin bed, using a bed sheet as a blanket. Frank, who had slept in the narrow space between the bed and the wall, rolled over and gave him a sour look.

"That," Joe said, "was the lousiest night's sleep I've ever had. Are you sure that sleeping on the floor is really an old tradition at science fiction conventions, Brian?"

Brian sat up slowly. "Sure it is," he said between yawns. "Of course, going seventy-two hours without sleep is also an old science fiction fan tradition."

"We're getting there," Frank said, standing up and stretching. "I spent half the night staring at the ceiling and the other half staring at my watch."

100

Chet, who had slept on the couch, got to his feet. "Let's go get some breakfast," he suggested.

Joe looked around the room. "By the way, Brian," he asked. "What happened to your uncle Pete?"

"He got up early and headed out," Brian said. "Didn't you notice?"

"I can't believe it," Joe said. "I must have actually been sleeping."

An hour later, after they had showered and eaten a quick breakfast, Brian and Chet left to attend a panel discussion. Frank and Joe stopped by the huckster room, where they found a dealer selling toy guns like the one that had been used to shoot at Simon Devoreaux on Friday evening. The dealer had no idea how anyone could have slipped a pistol inside one of his guns.

By late morning Joe was beginning to get discouraged as he and Frank wandered through the motel lobby and down the hallways. They had come up with no new theories and had found no new evidence.

As Joe passed a small room, he noticed a dim flickering of light visible through a small window in the door. Curious, he walked up to the door and peered inside.

What he saw startled him. "Well, what do you know," he said, squinting into the darkness. "Pete Amchick's in there—with Simon Devoreaux."

Frank crowded in beside his brother for a glimpse through the window. "Well, Amchick finally got to talk to Devoreaux."

101

"Do you think we should leave those two in there together?" Joe asked. "If Amchick's the one who's been trying to kill Devoreaux, it's probably not a good idea to leave them alone."

"They're not alone," Frank said, peering through the window. "I can see Devoreaux's bodyguards in there, too, sitting in the shadows."

"Amchick's showing Devoreaux some kind of movie," Joe said. "Can you make out what it is?"

"I can't see it any better than you," Frank said, "but I think it's the same film that Amchick was showing in the auditorium yesterday. The one that he made on a computer."

"So that's why Amchick has been chasing down Simon Devoreaux," Joe said. "He wanted to show him that film. I wonder why?"

"Maybe he wants to get a job as a special-effects director," Frank said.

"Somehow I can't see it," Joe said. "Amchick doesn't look the type. Besides, if he's the one who tried to kill Devoreaux the other night, why would he want to bump off his prospective boss?"

"I don't know," Frank said. "But we'd still better keep our eye on Amchick. Devoreaux might not be in any danger as long as the bodyguards are around, but we don't know what Amchick is up to."

"Okay," Joe said. "But—" He stopped in midsentence and turned away from the door. "Uh-oh. Look who just slithered in."

Joe pointed down the hallway, where George

Morwood was stepping out of an elevator. Morwood looked around nervously, then moved toward the lobby.

"He's acting kind of funny," Joe said. "I'll follow him and see what he's up to."

Frank nodded. "I'll stay here and keep an eye on Amchick and Devoreaux."

Leaving his brother, Joe followed Morwood into the lobby. Morwood headed out the door and rounded the building. Joe followed him quietly to the rear parking lot of the motel. He crouched down behind a parked car and watched as Morwood approached a man wearing a black leather jacket with chains hanging on it. They spoke for a minute, then headed for a small, windowless outbuilding behind the motel. As they opened a door and stepped inside, Joe left his hiding place and walked toward the brick building.

The door they had entered was marked No Admittance, and the building appeared to be some kind of storage room. Joe sat on the ground next to the building, hidden from the door by some thick bushes. Leaning his head against the bricks, he thought, I'll just wait here until they come out.

Joe was suddenly aware of how tired he was. After the long night on the floor of Brian's room, the lack of sleep was starting to catch up with him. Without realizing it, he closed his eyes and began to fall asleep.

Suddenly Joe's eyes snapped open, and he came

103

fully awake. He thought he heard a deafening bellow, like something out of an old jungle movie. He wondered if it had been a dream, but then he looked up and saw a huge object hovering over him.

Joe froze when he realized it was the foot of a large elephant, and that it was about to crush him into the pavement!

# 11 A Meeting in the Woods

Joe rolled aside just as the elephant's foot came crashing down on the pavement. He got to his feet and backed away from the huge animal. Joe winced as the elephant, which was still wearing the Surriband costume from the day before, made a bellowing noise and looked around as if deciding where to go next.

Joe's heart thumped loudly as he eyed the elephant nervously. Where in the world did this creature come from? he thought.

"There he is!" shouted a worried voice. Joe looked up to see a husky man in overalls racing toward the elephant. "Bruno! How did you get out of the tent?"

"Is . . . is this your elephant?" Joe asked.

"Yes, it is," the man in overalls said, a look of deep

concern on his face. "I work with the zoo. I brought this elephant here at the request of the people who do those Galactic Saga movies. They promised they'd keep him in their tent, but somehow he got away." He grasped the elephant's trunk. "Bad Bruno! Back to the tent."

"How did he get away?" Joe asked. "Didn't you have him tied up?"

"There was a metal chain attached to his leg," the man said, "but it had been unlocked. Someone must have let him loose."

"Why would they do that?" Joe asked. "He could have caused a lot of damage or gotten injured. Did you see anybody sneaking around the tent?"

"No," the man said. "I don't know who did this. It might have been somebody who thought they were doing Bruno a favor. People think elephants are so sweet and nice—and they're right. But one of these babies can crush a car with one foot. They should never be let loose around people. I have no idea why anybody would do that."

Joe looked up at the elephant's friendly face—or what was visible of it through the Surriband mask—and thought about how it had almost put a foot on his own face.

"Well, I hope you keep a close eye on him from now on," Joe said. "I'd hate to find myself, uh, getting underfoot again."

"I will, believe me," the man said. "I'm taking him back to the zoo right now. I should never have agreed to help these movie people."

The man led the elephant away. Joe looked after him, his heart still pounding. Suddenly limp, he sagged against the wall of the brick building and let himself calm down.

Joe took a deep breath and turned to look at the door where Morwood and the man in the leather jacket had disappeared. He saw that it was slightly open. Had Morwood left while he was asleep? he wondered. Joe eased open the door and looked inside. It appeared to be a grounds-keeper's shed, with rakes and shovels and other implements propped against the wall. There was no sign of either Morwood or the man Joe had seen him meet, and no clues to what they had been doing there.

Joe muttered angrily under his breath, "If only I'd gotten a better night's sleep, I wouldn't have dozed off waiting for Morwood to come back out." With a sigh, he walked back to the motel door, stepped inside, and headed to the hallway where he had left Frank.

Frank was still peering through the small window, looking a little bored. Joe came up beside him and glanced through the window.

"Morwood gave me the slip," Joe said in a frustrated tone. "How are things going here?"

"You're not going to believe this," Frank said, "but Amchick's showing Devoreaux that film for the third time. The director must really like it."

Suddenly the lights in the small room flickered on. "It looks as if that was the last showing," Joe said.

"They're starting to get up. We'd better make ourselves scarce."

Devoreaux and his companions began moving toward the door. Frank and Joe went a short distance down the hallway, in the opposite direction from the lobby, and watched them leave.

Devoreaux walked out of the room, followed by his bodyguards. When Pete Amchick came out, the director smiled and shook hands with him. They headed toward the lobby and out the front door.

"They're acting awfully friendly," Frank said.

"Maybe we were wrong about Amchick," Joe said. "He doesn't look like he's in the mood to kill Simon Devoreaux right now."

"Well, somebody stole that film and tried to kill both Devoreaux and Jack Gillis," Frank said. "If it wasn't Amchick, then it must have been either Morwood or Feinbetter. What happened when you followed Morwood?"

"He met some guy, and they went into a building behind the motel," Joe told him as he and his brother walked back toward the lobby. "I don't know what happened after that."

"Why didn't you wait until they came out of the building?" Frank asked.

"I fell asleep," Joe said.

Frank laughed. "Are you putting me on? My brother, the ace detective, fell asleep on the job?"

"You haven't heard the best part yet," Joe said with a grimace. He proceeded to tell his brother about the elephant.

Frank stopped short and shook his head in amazement. "Incredible," he said. "That story makes up for your unscheduled nap. I can't wait to hear what the gang at Mr. Pizza thinks of that one."

"They'll probably think I've flipped," Joe said. "But let's solve this case before we start telling stories about it, okay?"

As they continued down the hallway, they spotted Linda Klein, who was waiting for an elevator.

"Do you guys have any news yet?" she asked, a desperate tone in her voice. "I can't hold off giving Devoreaux that note much longer. Every time I have him convinced that he shouldn't sue us, something else happens."

"Relax," Frank said. "We're tracking down a hot lead. In fact, we'd better get going right now, before it gets away."

"Please," Linda said, wringing her hands, "move fast. I need you to solve this case as soon as you can."

After Linda Klein stepped into the elevator, Frank turned to Joe. "Now all we need is a hot lead," he said, "and what we just told Linda won't be a lie."

When they reached the lobby, Joe stopped short. "I see our hot lead now," he said, staring through the front window and into the parking lot. "Look."

Frank looked outside. In the parking lot he could see George Morwood, surrounded by several young men in leather jackets, one of whom was carrying a heavy-looking cardboard box.

"Who are those guys?" Frank asked.

"One of them is the guy I saw Morwood with

earlier," Joe said. "Maybe they're dealers in bootleg videotapes."

"They look more like a motorcycle gang to me," Frank said.

Morwood and his companions walked to the other side of the parking lot, then disappeared into the woods next to the lot.

"Want to follow them?" Joe asked.

"You have to ask?" Frank said. "Come on, let's go."

Frank and Joe left the motel and walked around the edge of the parking lot and into the woods. At the point where Morwood had entered the woods, Frank found a thin path that led between the trees and shrubs. The Hardys followed Morwood's trail, stepping lightly so that the leaves wouldn't make too much noise crunching underfoot.

When Frank saw Morwood and the group of men standing in a clearing, he held out a hand to Joe, signaling him to stop walking for a moment and observe what was happening. As they watched, one of the leather-jacketed men placed the box that he was carrying on the ground in front of Morwood. The video dealer bent down and picked up what looked to Frank like two unlabeled videotapes. Morwood glanced at them and then dropped them into the box. Then he pulled some money out of his pocket and handed it to one of the men in front of him.

"What do you suppose they're up to?" Frank asked in a low voice.

"I don't know," Joe said. "But it sure doesn't look very legal."

Suddenly Frank heard a crunching of leaves directly behind him. Before he could turn around, strong hands grabbed both of his arms. He struggled for a moment to get away, but he was being held in an iron grip. He craned his neck and saw that two of the men in leather jackets had come up behind him and grabbed him. Joe was also being held by two men.

"All right, you kids!" snapped the one at Frank's left elbow, a dark-haired man who looked as if he hadn't shaved in a week. "You better have a good story about what you're doing here, or this is the end of the line for you!"

# 12 Fatal Surprise

Frank struggled to break free, but his assailants gripped his arm more tightly.

"Let us go!" Joe shouted. "You can't do this to us."

"Look, you guys, we weren't doing anything wrong," Frank said quietly. "We were just going for a walk in the woods."

"That's right," Joe said. "We were getting a little tired of the convention and wanted some fresh air."

He saw George Morwood put down the box of videotapes he was examining and walk to the edge of the clearing to see what the commotion was about. "Oh, no," he said when he saw Frank and Joe. "Not you kids again."

"You know these kids?" one of the men asked from behind Frank's right ear.

"Yeah," Morwood said. "They've been hanging around this convention all weekend investigating a crime. They seem to think I was involved in it somehow."

The men laughed raucously. "Ha!" one of them said. "You wouldn't be involved with anything illegal, would you, Georgie-boy?"

"Knock it off," Morwood said, looking irritated. "I keep telling you guys, if anything shady is going on here, I don't want to know about it."

"Shady?" another of Morwood's companions said. "You know we'd never be involved with anything like that."

This comment set off another round of laughter. Finally one of the voices behind Frank asked Morwood, "What should we do with these kids? It looks like they were spying on us."

"Let them go," Morwood said.

"Let them go?" the voice said. "Are you crazy, George?"

"I don't think he sounds crazy at all," Joe said.

"It sounds like a really good idea," Frank agreed.

"These kids are harmless," Morwood said. "They're looking for the guy who stole Simon Devoreaux's film. That has nothing to do with me or you."

"Well, if you insist, George," the voice said. The arms holding Frank and Joe relaxed, and the brothers found themselves free again. Frank turned around to look at his attackers. They were two large men in leather jackets much like those of their companions. One had a broad, pudgy face, the other a chiseled profile. They glared at the Hardys with contempt.

Joe turned to George Morwood. "So what *is* going on here? It doesn't look very honest to me."

"Better watch what you say," the pudgy-faced man said menacingly. "We don't *have* to let you kids go."

"I'm just buying blank videotapes," Morwood said, gesturing toward the box at his feet. "I make videotapes of movies that aren't out in the stores."

"Bootleg tapes?" Frank said.

"No," Morwood said. "Perfectly legal tapes. I make deals with low-budget filmmakers to distribute their movies on video. I pay them a royalty on every copy sold. Some of these are films that never even get shown in the theater. Real small-time operations."

"And this is where you buy your blank tapes?" Joe asked. "In the middle of the woods?"

"That's right," Morwood said. "The profit margin on my business is very small. I can't afford to pay much for tapes. These gentlemen"—he indicated the men standing around him—"offer the lowest prices on blank tapes that I've been able to find."

"What were you doing earlier in the building in back of the motel?" Joe asked.

"So you kids *have* been spying on me," Morwood said. "I thought I noticed you snoozing outside the door when I came back out. I was just negotiating the deal before the tapes were delivered."

"Stolen tapes?" Frank suggested.

114

"I thought I told you kids to watch your mouths," the pudgy-faced man snarled, taking a step toward the Hardys.

"It's okay, Ron," Morwood said quickly, turning back to the Hardys. "I don't know where these tapes came from, and I don't want to know. It's none of my business. But I can assure you that I had nothing to do with the theft of Simon Devoreaux's movie. I don't get involved with things like that."

"Well," Frank continued, "I don't suppose you have any idea who it was."

Morwood shrugged. "I really don't. If that film is being bootlegged, I'll probably hear about it sooner or later. But I haven't heard a thing yet."

"If you do, give us a ring," Joe said.

"I'll do that," Morwood said. "Now, if you don't mind, I'd like to finish my transaction with these gentlemen."

Frank and Joe turned and walked past the men, who glared at them. When the Hardys reached the edge of the woods, they strode quickly across the parking lot back to the motel.

"That was a bad scene," Joe said.

"Yeah," Frank said. "I don't care much for Morwood's taste in business associates. You think those guys are honest businessmen?"

"Right," Joe said with a laugh. "And I'm King Kong. There's no way those tapes weren't stolen. The real question is whether or not Morwood had anything to do with the theft of Devoreaux's film."

"Well, he claims he didn't," Frank said. "And his

story about producing videotapes of low-budget films explains why he had those hand-labeled tapes under his counter."

"That still doesn't let him off the hook, though," Joe said. "But we don't have any evidence on him, so maybe we'd better concentrate on somebody else for a while."

"I still think we should talk with Devoreaux," Frank said. "He's at the center of all of this, and we haven't been able to get near him. He might be able to give us some helpful information."

"There's something else that's bothering me," Joe said as they stepped back into the lobby of the motel.

"Yeah?" Frank asked. "What is it?"

"That elephant that tried to squash my skull earlier," he said. "Who let it out of the tent?"

"I don't know," Frank said. "But whoever did it was probably trying to get you off the case— permanently."

"Whoever did it must have noticed me sleeping by the outbuilding," Joe said, "then led the elephant around to where I was lying. He probably left in a hurry when I woke up. So the question is, who would have the key to unlock the chain that was holding the elephant in the tent?"

"I don't know," said Frank. "I—"

"Hi, guys!" Brian Amchick said, coming out of the elevator. "How's the case going?"

"Not as well as we'd like," Frank said. "We were wondering if there might be some way we could get

116

to talk with Simon Devoreaux. You wouldn't happen to know where he is, would you?"

"As a matter of fact, I saw him in the coffee shop a little while ago," Brian said. "He might still be there."

"This may be our chance," Joe said. "Let's try to talk to him before he leaves."

Frank led the way back to the coffee shop, where they had eaten breakfast earlier. It was lunchtime, and the restaurant was nearly full. Simon Devoreaux and his bodyguards were sitting at a large table near the window. Frank approached the table, Brian and Joe immediately behind him, but one of the bodyguards stood up and blocked their path.

"We'd like to talk with Mr. Devoreaux," Frank said as the bodyguard turned a hostile gaze on him.

"So would a lot of people," the bodyguard said, folding his arms across his massive chest. "But Mr. Devoreaux doesn't want company. So get lost."

"It's about his stolen film," Joe said. "We're the detectives Linda Klein hired to find it, and it would be useful if we could ask him a couple of questions."

"Mr. Devoreaux has already spoken to the police about the missing film," the bodyguard said. "He doesn't need to talk to any kids like you about it. So, like I said, get lost."

Frank started to say something in reply, but suddenly there was a noise from the table where Devoreaux was speaking. Frank looked over to see the film director sit up halfway in his seat and make a desperate, gasping noise, his hands around his neck. Then the director collapsed in his chair, his face falling forward into the salad plate in front of him.

"What's wrong with him?" Joe asked.

Frank looked alarmed. "It doesn't look good."

Frank watched as the bodyguard seated next to Devoreaux lifted the director's face up and placed his hand against the unconscious man's neck. The bodyguard looked up with a troubled expression in his eyes.

"I think he's dead!" he cried.

# 13 Invader from Mars

"Dead?" Joe said in a shocked tone.

Just then he heard a voice from across the room shout, "I'm a doctor!" A man in a loose-fitting jogging suit hurried over to the director's table. He picked up Devoreaux's wrist and felt for his pulse.

"He's not dead," the doctor said finally. "But his pulse is very weak. Somebody call an ambulance immediately!"

The doctor reached down and picked up Devoreaux's plate. He held it under his nose and sniffed gently.

"This smells odd," he said. "It may have been poisoned. I'd recommend that nobody else eat anything until the food's been checked out."

Joe heard at least a dozen forks clank down

simultaneously around the room after the doctor had spoken. "Let's hope this doesn't turn into an epidemic," Joe whispered to his brother.

"This is terrible," Brian said, coming up behind the Hardys. "The convention is going to have a bad reputation after this."

"Let's just hope the ambulance gets here in time," Frank said.

"Somebody's been trying to ruin Devoreaux's health all weekend. It looks as if they've finally succeeded."

Within five minutes an emergency crew arrived. Joe watched as the paramedics examined Devoreaux for a moment, gave him an injection, and strapped him to a stretcher. Then they carried him out of the cafeteria. Joe caught a glimpse of Devoreaux's face as he left. It looked white and pasty.

"This has *not* been a good weekend," Joe said with a sigh.

"We've still got a case to solve," Frank said. He looked across the room to see Jack Gillis staring down at his salad plate. The Hardys walked over to say a few words to him.

"Excuse me, Mr. Gillis," Frank said. "We just wanted to say how sorry we were that this had to happen to Mr. Devoreaux."

"Hmmm?" Gillis looked up from his plate. "Oh, yes. You're the two boys who are investigating the theft. Thanks for the kind words. I'm pretty shaken up by what just happened to Simon."

"I'd be careful if I were you, Mr. Gillis," Joe said.

"Remember that somebody may be trying to harm you, too."

Gillis looked down at his plate again. "Maybe I'd better not eat any more of this. Not after what happened to poor Simon."

"Good idea," Frank said. "In fact, you might want to eat canned food for the rest of the weekend."

"Yes," Gillis said distractedly. "Well, I'll be packing up and heading back to Hollywood soon. I've got to get back out to the tent and start preparing the props for the trip back. If you'll excuse me . . ."

Joe watched Gillis stand up and walk away. Then he noticed a small black object that the special-effects director had left on his table.

"Hey, what's this?" Joe said. He reached down and picked up the object. "Gillis must have forgotten it."

Joe turned and called out Gillis's name, but he had already left the coffee shop. Joe shrugged and held up the object to examine it.

"What is it?" Frank asked.

"Some sort of electronic gadget," Joe said. "It looks sort of like the remote control for our VCR."

Joe turned it over in his hands. It was made out of black plastic in a rectangular shape and measured about five inches by two inches. There were several buttons on one side of it, with markings beneath them. Joe jabbed several of the buttons at random.

"Look out," Frank said. "You may have just launched a flight of missiles somewhere in Omaha."

"Why do I doubt that?" Joe said. "Well, we'll just

121

have to give this back to Gillis the next time we see him." He stuffed the device into his shirt pocket and turned back to his brother.

"There's nothing else to do here," Frank said. "Let's go check out some other leads. Maybe we can find Feinbetter and his friend Hennessy."

"Lead on," Joe said.

As the Hardys exited the coffee shop, they noticed several solemn-faced people wandering around outside.

"Word must be getting around about what happened to Simon Devoreaux," Joe said. "That ought to put a real damper on the convention."

As they stepped into the hallway, Joe heard the sound of raucous laughter. He turned to see two men with wide smiles on their faces happily slapping each other on the back.

"Well, speak of the devil," said Frank. "Richard Feinbetter and Arlen Hennessy. Wonder what they're so happy about?"

Feinbetter looked up to see the Hardys standing in front of them. "Well, hello, boys," he said jovially. "Have you heard the news?"

"You mean about Simon Devoreaux?" Frank asked.

"Yeah, that was the news," Hennessy said.

"I don't believe you guys," Joe said. "Are you laughing because Simon Devoreaux just got hauled off to the hospital?"

"Simon Devoreaux got what was coming to him,"

Feinbetter said. "That fraud has been making a fortune off my ideas for nearly ten years now, and I feel no sympathy for him at all."

Arlen Hennessy stopped laughing. "Maybe the kid's right, Rich. Devoreaux's treated you pretty badly over the years, but he didn't deserve to get poisoned."

"Mr. Feinbetter doesn't seem to agree," Frank said. "Do you, Mr. Feinbetter?"

"You're still wondering if I had something to do with the attacks on Devoreaux, aren't you?" Feinbetter said. "Well, I didn't. I'm not sorry that any of it happened, but it wasn't my doing. That's not my style."

"What *is* your style, Mr. Feinbetter?" Joe asked. "Stealing films?"

Feinbetter gave Hennessy a dirty look. "You should never have made that joke about me and the films, Arlen," he told him. "These boys aren't going to let up until they find the real culprit. Which I hope happens soon."

"I don't suppose you have an alibi for what you were doing when Mr. Devoreaux got poisoned, do you, Mr. Feinbetter?" Frank asked.

"As a matter of fact, I do," Feinbetter said. "For the last two hours I've been in one of the conference rooms delivering my guest-of-honor speech. And I have over one hundred witnesses. In fact, I just got out."

"Can't get a better alibi than that," Hennessy said.

"And I was there with him the whole time. So don't start getting any ideas that I might have had something to do with what happened to Devoreaux."

Hennessy nodded at Frank and Joe. Then he and Feinbetter turned and walked away.

"He's got us there, Joe," Frank said.

Joe sighed. "I guess so. But if Feinbetter didn't do it, who did?"

"Morwood isn't off the hook yet," Frank reminded his brother. "And neither is Pete Amchick."

"Yeah, but something's bugging me about all of this," Joe said. "I'm not sure what it is, though." He shrugged. "I'm starting to get a little stale. Maybe if we get our minds off this thing for a minute, we'll start getting some ideas."

"I saw something in the program about a room where they're showing movies," Frank said. "They had some neat stuff on the schedule. Maybe a half hour of old films will clear the cobwebs out of our brains."

"That's it over there," Joe said, pointing across the hall from the coffee shop at a sign that read, *Baru the Jungle Boy vs. the Martians:* Special Showing. Two metal spears had been propped in front of the sign as decoration. Next to the sign was a meeting room.

Frank opened the door and entered the room with his brother. It was dark inside, except for the flickering of a movie projector and an old black-and-white film showing on a screen at one end of the room. Several rows of chairs had been set up, and a few scattered fans were sitting in them. Frank found his way to the second row and sat down with his brother.

The film was mindless and silly, but Frank had to admit it was a lot of fun. A young boy who had been raised by apes in the jungle was battling against midget-size invaders from Mars. Frank watched along with his brother for about fifteen minutes, laughing at the dated dialogue and absurd plot twists.

"This is great," Joe said finally, "but we'd better get out of here and back on the case."

"Okay," Frank said, standing up. "Let's go."

On the screen a native tribesman in an elaborate headdress was preparing to throw a spear at one of the Martians. He cocked back his arm and prepared to launch the spear into the air.

As he threw it, there was a ripping noise from the screen. Frank, looking up in astonishment, realized that a real spear had come leaping out of the screen— and it was headed straight toward him!

# 14 The Magic Box

Frank twisted aside just in time. The spear landed right in the middle of the chair in which he had been sitting.

Joe looked at his brother in amazement. "Is that what I think it is?"

"Yeah," Frank said. "A spear. Straight from the jungle to my seat."

"Down in front!" somebody behind Joe shouted. "I can't see the screen."

"You can't see the screen because there's a big hole in it," another voice replied. "Somebody turn on the lights."

A moment later the room was flooded with light. The projectionist, a slender young man, turned off the film, and the image vanished from the screen.

"Wow!" exclaimed a boy in the row directly behind the Hardys. He stared at the spear that jutted up from Frank's seat. "This is better than three-D movies."

"A lot more dangerous, too," Joe said.

"Who would do such a crazy thing?" Frank asked, looking down at the spear embedded in the seat next to him.

Joe gazed up at the gaping hole in the middle of the screen. "There still could be somebody behind there," Joe said, pointing. He raced to the screen and looked behind it, but nobody was in sight.

"He would have gotten away by now," Frank said. He turned back to the projectionist. "Did you see anybody leave this room after that spear was thrown?"

"Yeah," the projectionist said. "Some guy just rushed out the door."

"Did you see what he looked like?" Joe asked.

"No," the projectionist said. "The lights were still out. All I saw was a silhouette when he ran into the hallway."

"Come on," Frank said. "Maybe we can still catch him."

Frank and Joe hurried into the hallway and looked around, but there was no one in sight. When Frank glanced back at the door to the room, however, he noticed that one of the spears that had been part of the display was missing.

"Well, we know where he got the spear," Joe said.

"Great," Frank said. "But that doesn't help us. We still don't know who threw it."

A light seemed to switch on in Joe's eyes. "Wait a minute!" he cried, grabbing his brother's arm. "I just realized something. There's a common thread running through a lot of the events that have taken place this weekend: the lightning bolt that almost hit Devoreaux, the phony elevator I walked through, the smoke bomb thrown by the costumed sorcerer, even that spear that jumped out of the movie screen."

"Yeah," Frank said. "They're all a lot weirder than the stuff we normally run into."

Joe shook his head. "They're all special effects—like you'd find in the movies. And not everyone here has the know-how to create special effects," Joe continued.

"Jack Gillis?" Frank suggested. "But somebody tried to *kill* Gillis yesterday afternoon. We were there, remember?"

"I know," Joe said. "But Gillis seems to be the most likely suspect."

"What about Pete Amchick?" Frank said. "He knows enough about electronics to pull off a lot of this stuff."

"True," Joe said. "But remember how I was wondering earlier who would have a key to let that elephant loose? Gillis would have one, and Pete Amchick wouldn't. Pete Amchick has the technical know-how to build that electrical contraption that almost zapped Simon Devoreaux last night, but I'm betting it's Gillis."

128

"And Gillis was in the restaurant while Devoreaux was eating," Frank said. "He could have gone over to Devoreaux's table to say a few words to him and secretly dropped something into his salad."

"There's one thing I can't figure, though," Joe said.

"What's that?" Frank asked.

"Why would Gillis steal his own film?" Joe said. "He said himself that he was co-creator of the movie. Why would he want to get rid of all the copies? For that matter, why would he want to kill Simon Devoreaux?"

"I don't know," Frank said. "But I think maybe we'd better have another conversation with Jack Gillis."

"Sounds good," Joe said. "Where do you think he is?"

"He told us he was going back out to the tent to get the props ready to ship back to Hollywood," Frank said. "Let's look for him there."

Frank and Joe walked back to the lobby. When they reached the parking lot, they could see the large green tent, but the flap was closed, and nobody appeared to be around.

Joe walked to the entrance of the tent. There was no place to knock, so he called Gillis's name instead.

"Mr. Gillis?" Joe shouted. "Are you in there? We have to talk to you for a minute."

There was no answer. Joe called Gillis's name again, but no one opened the flap.

"Maybe we should invite ourselves in," Frank suggested.

"Fine with me," Joe said. "It shouldn't be hard to open the flap. It looks as if Gillis left it unlatched."

Joe grabbed the edge of the flap and pulled it away from the canvas behind it. He looked inside. The exhibit was still set up the way he remembered it from the day before. Apparently, Gillis had not yet begun to disassemble it for the trip back. The two hovercars sat about ten feet away from Joe.

"Gillis doesn't appear to be around," Joe said.

"Let's wait for him awhile," Frank said. "He'll probably be back soon. The fact that he left the tent open probably means he wasn't going away for long."

Frank opened the flap and stepped inside the tent. "Where did this trunk come from?" he asked, pointing at a long, black trunk sitting in the middle of the tent. "It wasn't here yesterday."

"Maybe it's got more movie stuff inside it," Joe said.

"Let's take a look," Frank said. He knelt down in front of the trunk, popped open the latches, then lifted the top.

His pulse leaped. Inside the trunk were several costumes, including a sorcerer's robe, an astronaut's space suit, and a porcupine outfit. And on top of the pile was a green medallion with the moon and a star on it.

"This is incredible," Frank said. "Whoever put this stuff here is the same person who tried to kill Devoreaux."

"And who tried to kill me, too," Joe said. "Do you think this trunk belongs to Gillis?"

"It makes sense," Frank said. "Gillis seems to be running the whole show inside this tent."

"That clinches it," Joe said. "We're definitely going to have to talk to this guy again."

"Hey," Frank said suddenly. "What about that gadget Gillis dropped in the cafeteria? Do you think that might have anything to do with the case?"

"I don't know," Joe said, pulling it back out of his shirt pocket. "I don't have the slightest idea what it does."

He poked at a couple of buttons on the rectangular device. Suddenly the hovercar inside the tent began to move. Its fan started whirring, and it lifted about a foot into the air.

"What?" Joe exclaimed. "The hovercar just started up."

"Maybe—" Frank started to say.

Joe jabbed at another button on the little black box. To his amazement, the hovercar started moving forward, at full speed.

And this time it was heading straight toward Joe!

# 15 Over the Edge

"Get out of the way!" Frank shouted, leaping back through the flap of the tent as the hovercar hurtled toward them.

"Not yet!" Joe cried, holding out the black box in front of him, ready to dive rapidly to one side. He jabbed a button on the box, and the hovercar came to an immediate stop, about two feet in front of him.

Frank walked cautiously back into the tent and saw with relief that his brother was unharmed. "You're nuts, Joe! That thing could have flattened you. That car isn't science fiction—it's the real thing."

"Well, I knew what I was doing," Joe replied.

"What happened?" Frank asked. "What did you do?"

"We were right," Joe said, holding up the black

gadget. "This thing is a remote-control device. It operates the hovercars. When I pressed a button, the car started. All I had to do to stop it was to press the same button a second time."

"But I thought Gillis said there wasn't a remote control for this thing," Frank said. "He told us that it could only be operated by the driver."

"He was lying," Joe said, holding the remote control out to Frank. "He obviously didn't want us to know that this thing existed."

Frank snapped his fingers. "So that's what he used to operate the car yesterday when it almost ran him down."

"Right," Joe said. "He set up an attempt on his life to throw us off his trail. You thought you saved his life by pushing him out of the way, but actually he could have stopped the car at any time. He must have been carrying the remote control in his pocket."

"And he lied about it so we wouldn't figure that out," Frank said. "It all fits!"

"But we still don't know why he did it," Joe said. "Why did he take the film and try to kill Devoreaux?"

"I don't know," Frank said. "But I think we'd better find Gillis fast. He probably has the film stashed away someplace and plans to leave town with it as soon as he gets the chance."

"Let's look for him now," Joe said, stepping to the flap of the tent. Stopping short, Joe put his hand out to signal his brother, then whispered, "Wait a minute. I think I see him."

Joe pointed to the parking lot. Gillis was placing brown grocery bags in the trunk of a car.

"Think the film is in one of those bags?" Frank asked quietly. "And maybe the master negative, too?"

"Hard to tell," Joe said. "Let's go talk to him."

They walked over to Gillis. When he saw them approach, the special-effects director hastily closed the trunk.

"Good afternoon, Mr. Gillis," Joe said. "Good to see you again."

"Always glad to see you boys," Gillis said warily, "but I'm afraid I'm a little busy at the moment. Would you mind if I spoke to you later?"

"Actually, we would mind, Mr. Gillis," Frank said. "We need to ask you a couple of questions."

"For instance," Joe said, "what was that you were putting in the back of that car?"

"What?" Gillis snapped. "Why, my luggage, of course. I'm heading to the airport in a couple of hours."

"It didn't look like luggage to me," Frank said. "It looked like brown paper bags."

"I sometimes bring things to the convention in bags," Gillis said, glaring at the Hardys defensively. "These bags contain some props I was going to show the fans on Friday night. Before the film got stolen."

"Would you mind if we looked at them?" Joe asked.

"Yes, I would mind," Gillis said shortly. "And I'd

appreciate it if you boys would let me get back to my packing."

"Why did you lie to us about this remote control, Mr. Gillis?" Joe asked, holding up the little black box. "You said there was no way to control the hovercar at a distance."

"Where did you get that?" Gillis asked, his eyes widening in surprise. "I never let anyone touch that!" The special-effects man patted his coat pockets, as if he didn't realize he'd lost the remote control until the Hardys showed it to him.

"You left it in the coffee shop," Frank said. "We were going to bring it back to you . . . until we realized what it was."

Gillis's ruddy complexion turned a bright scarlet. "Give that to me!" he shouted, reaching out for the remote control. "That's a dangerous device. You could cause a lot of trouble with it."

"You faked that attempt on your life yesterday afternoon, didn't you?" Frank said. "You caused the hovercar to come rushing at you."

"You can't prove that," Gillis said. He grabbed at the device as Joe held it out of reach. The key chain Gillis had been holding fell out of his hand, and Frank snatched it off the pavement.

"Give me the keys!" Gillis cried, lunging toward Frank.

Joe grabbed Gillis by the arm as Frank stabbed one of the keys into the lock on Gillis's trunk. He popped the trunk open, reached into one of the paper bags, and pulled out a film canister.

135

"The stolen film," Frank said triumphantly.

"Let go of that," Gillis snarled.

"This is stolen merchandise," Frank said sternly. "If I gave it back to you, I'd be aiding and abetting a felony."

"It's not stolen!" Gillis cried. "That's *my* film. I was responsible for its creation."

"Tell that to Simon Devoreaux," Frank said.

"It's Simon Devoreaux who's the thief," Gillis said. "Not me."

"What?" Joe said. "I'm not sure I follow that."

"Simon Devoreaux stole the Galactic Saga from me," Gillis said. "Years ago. The entire series of films was my idea, not his."

"Funny—Richard Feinbetter claims that it was his idea," Joe said.

"Feinbetter?" Gillis said. "That old fool? I would never even read those books of his. Neither would Devoreaux. The resemblance to his books really was coincidence, just as we said in court. I conceived the idea for the films entirely on my own and brought it to Simon. He bought my idea on the spot. I thought we were going to share directing credit for it, but instead Simon got all the glory, pushing my name way down in the credits."

"You're pretty well known in the science fiction community," Frank said. "A lot of the people at this con have heard of you."

"That makes me a big fish in a very small pond," Gillis said with a sneer. "Devoreaux grabbed all the glory in Hollywood. He earns ten times what I do, and he's ten times more famous. If I'd known it would end up like this, I'd have gone to a different director.

"And to add insult to injury, Simon has decided to discontinue the series," Gillis continued. "*The Secret of Sigma Seven* is the final movie. And he's planning to start a new series—but without my special effects."

"Without your effects?" Joe asked. "How can he do that? His movies would be nothing without them."

"I agree with you completely," Gillis said. "But he's planning to hire a new special-effects director who will do everything entirely by computer. He saw a sample of this . . . this person's work and decided to talk to the man here at the convention. I heard the guy has found a way to do computerized special effects quickly and cheaply. No more scale models and camera tricks. Everything will be computer programs now."

"Pete Amchick!" Joe exclaimed. "Brian's uncle."

"Yes, I think that was his name," Gillis said. "Simon wanted him for the job because he wouldn't keep pressing him for proper credit, the way I did. And he'd work a lot cheaper, too. Devoreaux hasn't told me all of this yet, of course, because he wanted to meet with this Amchick person first. But I know what he plans to do. I've known Simon a long time, and I can read him like a book."

"So you decided to kill Devoreaux in revenge," Frank said. "But why steal the film?"

137

"Because if all the copies of the film were gone," Gillis said, "it would have to be filmed again. That's why I lifted the master negative before I left Hollywood, though it took them long enough to notice it was gone." Gillis smirked. "If the film needed to be remade, I'd be the perfect man to direct it. I'd offer my services to the studio and would finally get the proper credit for the Galactic Saga films. *I* would be the director."

Gillis sighed and went on. "And then you kids got into the act. I heard Friday night that you'd been hired by that Klein woman to snoop around the convention. I suspected you'd be trouble. I knew who you were when I saw you asking questions at the con party. You were already asking more questions than the police. So I tried to get you out of the way, too, but I never quite succeeded."

"You pulled some pretty fancy tricks," Joe said. "Like letting that elephant loose and rigging up that elevator door."

"Child's play," Gillis said with a shrug. "It was just good luck that the elevator was out of order. A little creative wiring had you fooled."

"What about that spear you stuck through the movie screen?" Frank asked. "How'd you manage it?"

"That was one of my favorite movies when I was a kid," Gillis said with a wry smile. "I used to have it memorized. I sneaked in right after you entered and hid behind the screen, waiting for the moment when I knew that the native would be throwing the spear. I

138

always like to do things with style. That's why I've gone as far as I have in my profession."

"One thing I really don't understand," Joe said, "is why you were always wearing that green medallion when you were in costume. Weren't you afraid that would give you away?"

"Not really," Gillis said. "I wanted you two to waste your time chasing disguised characters. There was no way you could tie the medallion to me. It was just a way to keep you busy while I finished off Devoreaux."

"You almost finished off Joe and me a couple of times too," Frank said.

"But you weren't clever enough to do it," Joe added. "I guess your effects weren't all that special." Joe and Frank looked at each other and laughed.

"Well," Gillis said, seeing that neither Frank nor Joe was watching him, "you never know when I might get another chance." His hand suddenly darted down into the dark trunk behind him and pulled out a large object.

Frank stared at Gillis in amazement as the special-effects director pointed a futuristic-looking gun at him and pulled the trigger. A thick ball of orange paint popped out of the muzzle. Before Frank could raise a hand to block it, it splattered all over his face.

"Hey!" Joe cried as Gillis fired a second paint ball at him.

Frank groped at his paint-covered face with his hands. "I can't see! That thing blinded me."

He pulled a tissue from his pocket and wiped the

paint out of his eyes. When he could see again, Gillis was nowhere around. But suddenly there was the whine of a hovercar fan, and one of the flying vehicles leaped out of the tent, with Gillis at the wheel.

"Here he comes!" Joe said as he wiped the paint from his face.

"And he's headed right at us!" Frank shouted.

The brothers ducked, and the hovercar zoomed over them. Gillis rocketed off toward the parking lot exit.

"He's getting away," Frank said. "Use the remote control. Quick!"

Joe pointed the remote control toward the escaping hovercar and pressed the buttons desperately, but nothing happened. "No good," he said. "Gillis must have some way to override the remote from inside the car."

"Then we'd better find a car and start chasing him," Frank said. "But our van's all the way on the other side of the lot."

Frank heard a whining noise from the tent and turned to see the second hovercar come rushing out through the tent flap.

Joe grinned. "Whoa," he said, pushing the button on his remote to make it stop. "I guess the other car heard my signal."

"Way to go," Frank said, leaping into the hovercar. "Get in, and let's follow Gillis."

Joe jumped into the hovercar after his brother. "Good thing Gillis showed me how to operate this

140

thing!" he shouted. "I didn't think my hovercar driving lessons would come in handy quite this soon."

Joe pushed the joystick forward, and the hovercar rushed across the parking lot. He pushed it toward the exit as Gillis raced away in the distance.

The special-effects director was about a hundred feet ahead of the Hardys as Joe steered the hovercar onto the street that ran past the motel. As they hit the open road, it was obvious that the hovercars couldn't move as quickly as normal automobiles.

"If we had an ordinary car, we'd be able to chase Gillis down more easily," Joe said.

"Just stay on his tail," Frank said. "He's got to stop eventually."

"I just hope he doesn't take that thing into heavy traffic," Joe said. "I don't know if I can steer this thing around real cars."

As if he had heard Joe's statement, Gillis turned off the narrow road he was on and guided his hovercar onto a four-lane highway. As he did, he almost collided with a van. The van skidded to a halt, and the driver honked his horn loudly.

"Oh, boy," Frank said. "This is going to be a real mess."

Joe followed Gillis as he continued down the highway, with drivers honking their horns and gawking in disbelief. Where in the world is Gillis going? Joe wondered as the special-effects director weaved his car back and forth between lanes to avoid traffic jams.

"Where's he headed?" Frank asked.

"That's what I was wondering," Joe said. "I doubt that even he knows. He's not from Bayport, so he can't know his way around very well. We could end up anywhere."

"I hope we end up in the vicinity of a police car," Frank said. "Maybe if they stopped him for a ticket, we'd have a chance to catch up with him."

"What would they ticket him for?" Joe asked. "Wheels not in contact with the ground?"

"Yeah," Frank said. "Driving at a reckless altitude."

Joe swerved as Gillis turned off the highway and onto a road that led out of town.

"He's headed toward Barmet Bay," Frank said.

"And Barmet Cliffs," Joe said.

Sure enough, a series of white rocks appeared off the side of the road, with the blue of the bay visible beyond them. Gillis turned off the road and headed straight for the rocks.

"What's he doing?" Frank cried. "He's heading right for the cliffs!"

"I don't know," Joe said, "but we can't lose him now."

Gillis drove straight toward the rocks and, to Joe's amazement, went right over them. The hovercar disappeared below the cliffs and plunged toward the bay more than a hundred feet down.

"Oh, no," Frank said urgently. "He went over the edge. Stop the car, Joe. You don't want to follow him there."

142

"He never showed me how to stop this thing," Joe said frantically, searching the dashboard for the right button or lever. "I don't know where the brakes are!"

"Use the remote!" Frank cried.

Joe grabbed for the remote control in his jacket pocket, but it was too late. Before he could reach it, the hovercar went over the edge of the cliff and began falling straight down toward the water far below!

# 16 Splash Landing

Joe's stomach lurched as the hovercar plunged toward the bay. It was like being in an elevator with a
broken cable, he thought, except that this elevator
shaft had a view that must have stretched for fifty
miles in every direction. The rock walls of Barmet
Cliffs shot past at high speed as the water rapidly
rose toward him from below. Joe craned his neck
over the edge of the car to get a look down at the
water underneath—and immediately wished he
hadn't. The bright blue surface was coming up
awfully fast.

"The fans aren't doing anything to hold us in the
air anymore," Joe told his brother, trying to remain
calm.

"What do you think this is, a jet?" Frank shouted

in return. "This baby flies on a cushion of air, and now there's no ground to support the cushion!"

"Let's hope this thing works on water, too," Joe said, "or we're gonna be history."

Just as it looked as though they were about to plunge into Barmet Bay, the air pressure kicked in again, like a parachute opening at the last second. Joe felt the hovercar hit the water with a solid *whomp* that almost knocked him out of his seat, and then he realized that the car was floating two feet above the water. He looked down and saw the whirring fans stir up a bowl-shaped basin of water directly underneath him. "We're in luck!" Joe exclaimed, wiping off the water that had splashed in his face.

"There he goes!" Frank shouted, pointing at Gillis's hovercar, which was already shooting out across the water ahead of them.

"Here we go again," Joe said, pushing the joystick in Gillis's direction. The hovercar shot forward across the water in pursuit of the fleeing special-effects director.

"This is great," Frank said. "I've always loved speedboat racing."

Suddenly Joe heard the sound of a boat engine off to their left. He turned to see a motorboat slicing across the water, foam spewing up in its wake. The driver was watching the Hardys' hovercar with astonishment.

"Uh-oh," Joe said, "I think that guy's too stunned by our hovercar to notice where he's going."

145

"He's headed straight for Gillis's hovercar," Frank added.

Gillis saw the speedboat coming, too. He yanked his joystick frantically to propel himself out of its path, but it was too late. As Joe watched, the speedboat plowed right into the side of Gillis's hovercar, ripping it neatly down the middle and sending Gillis flying high into the air. The special-effects director did a double flip and landed back in the water with a splash. The stunned speedboat pilot downshifted his engine and began turning in a circle, shaking his head as if he hoped that the past thirty seconds would turn out to be a bad dream.

"I hope Gillis didn't hit the water too hard," Joe said.

"Yeah," Frank said. "That speedboat really clobbered him. If that had happened on land, he'd be a goner for sure."

"There he is," Joe said, pointing into the waves stirred up by the crash. Gillis was bobbing back up to the surface, his arms flailing at the water around him.

"Help me!" he sputtered as the Hardys drew closer.

"Be glad to," Frank said as Joe slowed the speedboat down. "In fact, we'd be glad to help you all the way back to the Bayport Police Station."

A little while after they left Gillis with the police, Frank and Joe were sitting on the leather couches in the lobby of the Bayport Inn.

146

"So how did you figure out it was Gillis?" Brian Amchick asked. "I never dreamed it might be him."

"Oh, logical thinking and a few brilliant deductions," Joe said, lounging back on the comfortable sofa. "I mean, that's how we solve all of our cases, isn't it, Frank?"

"I thought it was usually dumb luck," Chet said, popping another taco chip into his mouth. "These things are great. I've got to go back up to the con suite and get some more."

"Well, I'm really impressed," Brian said. "If I ever need any detective work done, you guys will be the first people I'll call. By the way, you'll never guess what happened to my uncle this weekend."

"He got a job as Simon Devoreaux's new special-effects director," Frank stated.

Brian's eyes opened wide. "Yeah! How'd you guess?"

"Oh, just another brilliant deduction," Frank said with a grin. "All in a day's work for Joe and me."

"He told me all about it this afternoon," Brian said, leaning forward in his chair. "He couldn't talk about it before because the deal wasn't finalized, but now I can't shut him up. It seems that Devoreaux really did ask him to come here, but the plans got messed up because of all the weird incidents that were going on. Anyway, my uncle has developed this quick, cheaper way of doing special effects, and Devoreaux wants to use it in his films."

Linda Klein walked into the room and zeroed in on the couch where Frank and Joe were sitting.

147

"There you are!" she exclaimed, a beaming smile on her face. "I've been looking all over for you. I wanted to thank you for getting the film back. You've really saved my life."

"You're welcome, Linda," Frank said. "How's Simon doing?"

"The doctors say he's doing surprisingly well," Linda said. "Apparently, he didn't eat enough of the poisoned salad dressing to cause any serious damage. He'll be back making films in no time."

"My uncle will be relieved to hear that," Brian said.

"So I guess he won't be suing you guys when he's back up and around?" Joe asked.

"Nope," Linda said, smiling. "He was stunned when he found out that his own special-effects director was behind the theft and the attempts on his life. He couldn't have been more apologetic about the way he'd acted toward the people at the convention. In fact, he's even promised to premiere his next film at BayCon as soon as it's finished.

"Oh, by the way," she added, pushing her dark hair away, "I've got a message for you guys from somebody in the huckster room. A George Morwood. He's a dealer in videotapes."

"Right," Frank said. "We know him."

"He said to tell you that he's been thinking it over and has decided he's been dealing with the wrong business associates," she said. "From now on he's going strictly legitimate, whatever that means."

"Who would have guessed?" Joe said, looking at his brother.

"Maybe we shook George up a little after all," Frank said.

Chet crunched loudly on a taco chip. "You know, I think I've decided to become a full-time SF fan."

"Really?" Linda Klein asked. "Do you read a lot of science fiction, Chet?"

"No, I only see the movies," he said. He held up the bag of taco chips. "But I'm a fan of any place that gives out free food. Think I could buy an advance membership in next year's con?"

"Well, actually, we're thinking of charging a small amount for the food after this year," Linda said.

A surprised look crossed Chet's face. "Why?" he asked.

"It seems that somebody ate an amazing amount of taco chips at the con parties on Friday and Saturday nights," Linda said. "Frankly, we can't afford to supply enough food to keep up with the demand."

Frank laughed. "It looks as if you're going to have to cut down on your eating next time, Chet, or you're going to drive BayCon out of business."

"Chet cut down on his eating?" Joe said with a grin. "Now, *that's* science fiction!"

# NANCY DREW® MYSTERY STORIES  By Carolyn Keene

# THE HARDY BOYS® SERIES  By Franklin W. Dixon